Bought at "Mainstreet
August 9, 1996

Sweet Hollow

Stories by Lou V. Crabtree

Louisiana State University Press
Baton Rouge and London
1984

Library of Congress Cataloging in Publication Data

Crabtree, Lou V.
  Sweet Hollow.

  Contents: Homer-snake — Prices' bewitched cow — Little Jesus — [etc.]
  I. Title.
PS3553.R19S9 1984   813'.54   83-14934
ISBN 0-8071-1132-5
ISBN 0-8071-1133-3 (pbk.)

The author gratefully acknowledges permission to reprint
"Holy Spirit," which appeared in *Laurel Review*, copyright © 1981.

Fifth printing (April, 1992)

For
Lawrence Judson Reynolds
and
Lee Smith

Contents

Sweet Hollow

Homer-Snake

Old Marth claimed all the blacksnakes as hers. She tongue-lashed the roving Murray boys, who went into people's barns and caught snakes and took them by their tails and cracked them like whips. This cracking broke the body of the snake and sometimes snapped off its head. It was terrible to see the Murray boys wring a snake around a few times, then give a jerk and off snap the head.

Old Marth lived in her cabin next to our cabin down in the hollow of the river hills. She pinned her gray hair with long wire hairpins. I watched her stick the wire hairpins into her hair with little flicks of the wrist. It hurt her head, I thought. Only when she was bothered did her hair escape the pins and fall in gray wisps about her face. Bud, my brother younger than I a few years, thought it his mission in life to trail me, to spy, and to report on me to Maw. Some things Bud would tell but not many. Only things on me. Bud said I told everything I knew. Maw said it, too. Because of this, Bud never let me trek over the hills with him.

He said, "She just can't keep from talking. She talks all along the trace. If you talk, you don't get to know anything."

Old Marth leaned down close to Bud. "Blacksnakes are best of friends. Come down to my house and I'll show you Homer-snake."

I had seen Homer-snake many times. Bud had, too. Homer had lived for years back of Old Marth's house in the corner of the outside rock chimney. A hole was visible, where for warmth Homer crawled in the winter.

I once asked Old Marth, "Did Homer-snake dig his hole by himself?"

Old Marth replied, "I expect it is a once frog hole."

What Old Marth told Bud next was not news to Bud or to me. We had both seen it a million times.

"Homer-snake likes milk to drink. I put out milk for him in his saucer every day. Best of all he likes cream, which I don't give him but ever once in a while. He might get too fat to go in his hole." Old Marth laughed, then fiercelike advanced close to Bud. "Don't you ever come to be tormenting blacksnakes. I'll be wastin' my breath if you come to be like them rovin' Murray boys. Come to my house soon and get better acquainted with my Homer-snake."

Old Marth wouldn't have liked what Bud was carrying around in his pocket. I asked him what the small white rocks were that looked like they were rolled in salt.

"Blacksnake eggs. I found them under a rock up the ridge."

Old Marth was always asking me to go home with her to spend the night. She never asked Bud. He tried to devil me behind Old Marth's back.

"How would you like to turn down your bed covers and there would be Old Homer all curled up warming your bed?"

Then I accused Bud of being jealous, and we got into one of our many spats until Maw moved in, saying, "Old Marth just don't like boys. She is suspecting on account of them Murray boys."

Bud never was known to give up. He used to slink around the house as I was leaving, and peep around the corner, and hiss, "Don't sit down on Homer-snake."

Behind Old Marth's house and up a little rocky path was her vegetable garden. To one side was her little barn where she kept her cow, some hens, and a red rooster. The rooster did not like Homer and gave him many a good flogging. He raked Homer with his spurs until Homer fled from the barn, leaving the rooster and hens alone.

Nevertheless, on the sly, Homer would steal into the barn where he unhinged his jaws and swallowed whole one of the hen's nice eggs. Then off he would sneak, toward the rocky path, where he knocked and banged himself against the rocks until the prongs on his ribs crushed the shell of the egg. Once I saw Homer with a huge knot along his body, and I rushed to Old Marth, alarmed.

Old Marth answered in a knowing way. "Most likely an egg. Could be a mouse or a baby rabbit. Homer-snake is having his dinner."

Once the Murray boys were out "rogueing" — knocking off apples and stealing eggs. Homer was in the warm hen's nest where the hen had just laid a nice egg. Homer liked the warmth and was nestling down and warming himself before swallowing the egg, which was sort of an ordeal for him. A rude hand, reaching into the nest, and pulling out Homer, let go quickly. Even the Murray boys didn't like surprises like Homer.

"Homer is my protection," cackled Old Marth as the Murray boys skirted her place, skulking about carrying an old sack they put their loot into. Old Marth guessed that the Murray boys were out to get Homer. Twice they were almost successful.

Homer loved to climb trees. There were young birds and other delights. He played hide and seek up in the sycamore tree down by the little springhouse. He climbed to the very tiptop and out of his snake eyes viewed the world. I liked to watch him hang like a string and swing in the sycamore tree.

On this particular day, Old Homer had left the sycamore and was up in the tree that had the squirrel's nest. It had once been a crow's nest, but the squirrels had taken over for the summer. In the winter they had a fine home in a hole just below the crow's nest.

Homer liked young squirrels almost as much as young rabbits.

The Murray boys almost got Homer that time. They spotted him up in the tree that had the squirrel's nest. Climbing a tree was nothing to the Murray boys. They could climb to the top of any tree in the Hollow. Homer-snake was in a predicament. The leanest of the Murrays was coming right on up the tree with no problem. Homer couldn't see Old Marth anywhere. It would be too late in a minute. A rough hand would be reaching for him.

There were some small limbs, too small to hold the weight of a boy, and farther on, still smaller limbs that just possibly could hold up a snake. Out crawled Old Homer and with great care coiled himself round and round the smallest ones.

The Murray boy was plain mad. The limb would not hold up his weight. He ventured out as far as he could and leaned out and down and stretched his arm toward Homer.

"Shake him loose. Shake hard."

Round and round the tree looking up, calling louder and louder, went the rest of the boys until the red rooster brought together his pack of hens and they all set to cackling, which caused the hogs to trot around the pen, grunting. Just in time, out of the house, like a whirlwind, came Old Marth. The Murray boys knew to make themselves scarce and they hightailed it, except the one caught up in the tree who tried to skin down fast. Old Marth got hold of his hair and yanked him about, and when he left, he left a piece of his shirt with Old Marth.

Laughter floated backwards as the Murray boys hightailed it, putting distance between them and Old Marth's screeching.

"Rogues! Torments! Thieves!"

So Homer was saved this first time.

Another time, the Murray boys were watching Old Marth's house and knew she was away. They were walking around looking at the roots she had tied up to the rafters of her porch. They had been down to the hogpen and down to the springhouse and had drunk out of the gourd. They spied Homer, who was coming from the garden. He barely got halfway in his door when one of the Murrays got him by the tail, straining and tugging to pull him out. What they did not know was that no one, not anyone, can pull a snake out of his hole, once he gets part way in. The snake swells up and spreads his scales and each scale has a tiny muscle. The snake may be pulled into two parts, but he will never be moved. The Murray boys did not give up easy as they pulled and tugged.

"Pull harder. Yank him outa there."

Homer was about to come apart when he felt footsteps coming along on the ground. Old Marth, home early, came upon the scene and chased off the Murrays with a tongue-lashing they would remember. Homer-snake was saved the second time, but there was to be a third.

In the late summer, Homer got a new skin. He molted. He had a bad case of lassitude. Then his whole body was itching so he could not rest. His lips began to split and his eyes turned milky. He was milky-looking all over. He made trip after trip up into the garden, ate a big lunch of snails and bugs, and lazed back down over the rocky path.

One day there was his old skin beside the path in the rocks. Of course he knew all along what he was doing and just how to do it. He rubbed and rubbed himself against the rocks until his old skin loosened and he rolled it off wrong side out. Just like Bud shed his clothes.

Old Marth found the skin and tied it with several others to the rafters of her porch. When the wind rattled them, they scared me, but not Homer's old enemies, the Murrays.

Old Marth said to Bud after Homer shed his skin, "I will make you acquainted with the new Homer. Don't you like him? Ain't he handsome? Like a new gun barrel, he is."

With his new skin, Homer was so shiny and new, I think Bud almost liked him. Homer looked "spit shined," like Paw said about his shoes from his old army days.

Homer got along real well with the cow. She ignored him and never got ruffled if she came upon him suddenly. Homer only had to watch her feet. She did not care where she stepped. Four feet were a lot to watch and one day Homer got careless. One of the cow's feet came down hard on about three inches of Homer's tail. When Homer looked back, the end of his tail was broken off and sticking out of the mud in the cow's track. His beautiful tail. So for the rest of his life he went about trailing his blunted tail, and after a while he didn't seem to miss it.

Bud said, "I can always tell if it is Homer trailing through the sands and dust. Among the squiggles you can see where his old stepped-on tail went."

Down in the springhouse Old Homer guarded the milk crocks. He would curl around a crock like giving it a good hugging. Old Marth had to keep the lids weighted down with heavy rocks so Homer wouldn't knock the covers off and get in the milk.

Looking back, behind the springhouse, was a swath of daisies with bunches of red clover marked here and there, winding all the way to the top of the ridge. This swath was Homer-snake's special place. He liked to lie and rest and cool off among the daisies. He played all the way to the top of the ridge, got tired and slept, had lunch along the way, slithered down when he chose, spending the whole of a summer's day to arrive back home in the cool of the evening. The daisies gave Homer-snake a nice feeling.

The Murray boys were Homer's end. This was the third encounter.

"All things have an end." Maw said later.

Maw sent me down to Old Marth's place to swap some quilt pieces. Going to her house was all right if I could locate Homer. Sitting on Homer or having him swing down from a rafter and touch me on the shoulder never got any less upsetting. But something bad was waiting for us all that day at Old Marth's place.

Homer was fat and lazy and full of cream.

"I'll put in a spoon of jelly for you, Homer." Old Marth put the jelly in Homer-snake's saucer and went on her way. She was going over the hill to visit and take a sample of the jelly.

Homer loved the jelly. Then I know he began feeling lonely. Loneliness led to carelessness. He failed to notice that everything was too quiet. The birds were quiet like the Murray boys were in the vicinity. The chickens were quiet like a hawk was circling. Homer decided to slip past the rooster and go into the barn to rest.

The Murray boys were out "funning" all day all over the hills. They were stirring up bees' nests beside the trace and getting people stung. They were running the cows so they wouldn't let their milk down. They were riding the steers and tormenting the bull.

They saw Old Marth going over the ridge and grinned at each other and jammed down their old hats over their ears and hitched up their britches. Preparing themselves. Preparing to steal eggs out of the hens' nests, they went into the barn. Bud saw it all and told Maw.

Maw said to me, "There is such a thing as keeping your mouth shut."

Bud was watching the Murray boys that day. He had trailed them and watched from the far edge of the woods on the top of the hill. Bud was always watching. I saw him in the plum grove. He was no partner in what happened.

The Murray boys went into the barn with their everlasting sack, stayed a few minutes, rushed out toward the hogpen, pitched the sack, and whatever was in it, over to the hogs. Then they laughed and shouted and hightailed it.

I saw it. Bud saw it. I ran to tell Maw.

"They threw the sack and Homer in it into the hog pen. The hogs will eat up Homer." I was running, screaming wild, and blubbering.

I was so excited with telling the tale that I had not had time to feel sorry for Homer. The hogpen was one place Homer never fooled around. Even Homer knew that hogs ate up blacksnakes.

Bud had come up. "How are you going to keep her from blabbing?" Bud thought he was the world's best at keeping his mouth shut. He gloried in keeping secrets.

I wanted to talk about what I saw, and I wanted to bring it up ever afterwards and keep asking questions. There was so much to wonder about.

"She will tell her guts," Bud said.

"Let Homer bide," was what Maw said to me and meant it. I could tell for her mouth was a straight line across.

Old Marth came home, missed Homer, and looked everywhere. Bud and I stood around and watched her. Her eyes were on the ground looking for some sign, trying to find a trail.

I mooned around and was about sick seeing Old Marth with her graying hair stringing and wisping about her face. Until one day, Old Marth said, "If Homer were alive, he would show up. I know when to give up hopes. I resign myself."

Determined not to let anything slip about Homer, for a while, it helped to clap both hands over my mouth when questions began popping in my head. I didn't want ever to be the first one to tell about Homer being eaten by the — I must not say it now.

Maw kept saying, "Let it bide a while."

Old Marth came back to our house to churn. Her hair like a cap was pinned up with long hairpins. Maw required neat hair around the butter, for a hair found in the butter made a bad tale up and down the Hollow.

I kept holding both hands over my mouth to keep from telling until one day Old Marth noticed and said, "You are acting funny." Turning to Maw, she said, "The child is sick. Goes around all the time about to vommick holding her hands over her mouth. Just might be she is wormy and needs a dose."

I wasn't sick. Maw knew it. Bud knew it.

Days went by, to a day when I went down for a look in the hogpen. The hogs grunted, pointed their ears, and looked up at me with their little pig eyes close together.

There under the slop trough I saw it. The proof I was not seeking. I saw a piece of old sack. I screamed what the whole world already knew. "They threw the sack and Homer in it into the hogpen. The hogs ate up Old Homer." I leaned against the pen and I retched until I spit up. I was really sick. The hogs saw it. Bud did, too, for he was in the plum grove, spying as usual. I started running, jumped some puddles, got tired, and came to stop where some daisies covered with dust were beside the road.

I began feeling nice. The daisies were nice. Old Marth's place behind me was nice. Up overhead the fleecy sheep clouds stood stock still to become masses of daisies. Over to the left was a patch of red sky clover. Then the sheep clouds moved together and formed a maze and across the sky was a swath of daisies. Just like the swath Homer had traveled up the trace to the top of the ridge. I was delighted and looked a long while. I know I saw it. There placed in the maze of daisies he loved so well was Homer-snake. He stood upright on the end of his blunt tail and looking over the daisies, he laughed at me.

I laughed and went home.

Maw's kitchen was nice with smells of sassafras tea, spicewood, gingerroot, milk cheeseing, and cold mint water fresh from the spring.

Bud came in the door, reporting on me. "Maw, I saw her. She has been down to Old Marth's hogpen."

"Whatever for, child?"

Maw didn't expect an answer, and I had already turned my back on Bud. I felt something new in my life. The day was coming soon when I could handle Bud. Maw refers to it as _patience_. Patience was something Bud did not have. Bud hung around, waiting on me to start talking and telling everything. I sat until Bud gave up and left, then I told Maw, "I saw Old Homer-snake among the daises in the sky. He stood up on his blunt tail and laughed at me."

Maw left her dough-making and with flour up to her elbows, she took my head in both hands. "Precious. You saw what you hoped for, for Homer. Homer-snake is all right. You are all right. Find your little pan. You can come help me make up this bread."

Prices' Bewitched Cow

Do cows have spells like humans? Witchcraft, whimsey, or just plain lunacy? The hill people believe in witches. If asked about this, they will deny it. But they do. If people ask me, did I ever know a witch, I sure did. The most important kind — one who could break spells.

"A real good milker." Maw bragged about the gallons of rich yellow milk Old Nannie cow supplied to our table, as well as to the tables of our neighbors.

Witches played a part in Old Nannie cow's life. Born and bred in the river hills, Nannie was a common sort of cow. Just a plain yellow jersey with white markings under her belly. But strange things happen down in the hills where, of uncertain age, Nannie was, at times, a vagrant, taking to the knobs where she stayed for days. Did she consort with witches? Finally she came in home, her udder strutted to bursting, the streams of milk trailing to the ground.

"I saw a blacksnake trying to suck Old Nannie," reported Bud, whose job was driving the cow to the milkgap.

No one showed any surprise since everybody knew that blacksnakes pilot other snakes, that they drive cows, and that, smelling the milk, the blacksnakes suck the cows.

"Nannie cow looks a sight like Maw Price," observed Old Marth, poking in the wash kettle.

Old Marth was a woman who lived nearby and worked for Maw, doing the washing and churning, and in season, other chores.

It was the eyes. Maw's eyes, like Nannie cow's eyes, were thoughtful, even after it was all over, when Nannie became the same gentle yellow jersey, and the tale was put to rest by everyone except me.

Despite years of field work and childbirth, Maw's eyes just melted into you.

Old Marth mused out loud, "Yes, Nannie cow's eyes and Maw Price's eyes are the same — dark, thinking."

Maw had gone to the store. Should she be late returning, she had left Old Marth to do the milking and keep Bud and me company.

The evening was quiet. The sun still shone at home, but the shade had already come to the hollows. From a distance, the hollows between the hills looked black. Maw had not returned. Old Marth chewed on the stem of her clay pipe, trying it first on one side and changing it to the opposite one.

We sat upon the ground, Old Marth and I, to wait on Bud to bring in Nannie from the upper pasture, as the cows liked to stay next to the Hagy line where they could see the Hagy cows.

The silence was broken by the clanking of the cowbell. Old Marth held her pipe in her hand and we turned to look.

"Heavens. What is wrong with Nannie cow?"

We stood up. Nannie stood looking up the hill where, in the sage grass, a stump had burnt black, years before, in a fire.

"She's cutting a shine."

Nannie, dear old cow, had never taken the stump into notice. Now with her tail standing over her back, she was circling the stump, stomping her feet and bellowing, her eyes popping out of her head. She stood gazing at the stump, snorting and blowing. I could see nothing, but certainly Nannie did, the way she was bugging her eyes.

"Nothing there but an old black stump. Has a nest egg in it, so old it is rotten," said Old Marth who kept up with the hens' nests.

Never did I get brave enough to go close to the stump. A long time later Bud, who was venturesome, said the egg was there, discolored by age and weather.

Other cows came in to add to the excitement. Nannie watched the stump all night and part of the next day. All the cows moved about restless. At our approach they would throw up their heads and paw the ground. We did not milk that night or the next morning. As days passed and Nannie refused to pass the stump, we talked about changing the milkgap.

"Nannie saw the devil go into that stump."

Old Marth tied her apron tighter, preparing to go home. She was so afraid of the cow that she refused to come to our house anymore to do the milking and washing. This caused the milking to fall heavily on Bud and me.

So the tale on Nannie cow was started, which caused Nannie to become the most talked about cow down in the river hills.

They talked in the fields at the end of a row when they rested; they talked in their beds at night. Everybody knew about our cow. Tales were told of old tales they had heard, of how someone's grandmaw's cow had seen the devil and acted the same way.

"This won't be the end of it." Down at the meetinghouse they nodded their heads.

It wasn't. The stump part was just the beginning.

Maw had saved milk for a large churning. Bud and I were worn out. The milk would not churn butter. After backbreaking churning for nearly an hour, there was no butter. Just foam — foaming and running out the top of the churn, down the sides, onto the floor. I raised the lid and the foam rolled out. The milk kept foaming and foaming, like the little porridge pot that boiled and boiled and filled the room when the magic word was lost.

"Bud, say your magic word," I said.

Bud had a number of magic words he said over the hills, at old logs, at certain rocks and trees. Also, when he passed certain persons, he always crossed his fingers so if any bad luck spells were wished on him they were no good.

I tried crossing my fingers. Bud's charm did not work for me. The longer we churned the more milk we had. No end to it. It ran like a river over the floor. Maw became exasperated and her hair spilled over her face.

"Try pouring in some cold water. Maybe it is too hot."

"Try pouring in some hot water. Maybe it is too cold."

We churned some more. We churned long periods and we churned short periods. We tried everything and nothing helped. For weeks and weeks the same thing happened. We were vexed to a standstill as each churning came to just that. A standstill.

In the hills, no one could eat without butter. Hot biscuits and butter started off the morning right.

Time after time, we gave up on the churning, and the hogs got an extra feeding for we carried the milk out for slop.

Over the weeks, Maw tried six churnings. It was the seventh churning.

"Seven is a magic number," Bud said.

We both chanted, intoned, begged as we said together,

"Come butter. Come."

The result was no different.

Talk flared up again. People began to refer to Nannie cow as Prices' Bewitched Cow. They remembered that Nannie had seen the devil go into the black stump. People began searching their memories. There were recalls and exchanges. Someone remembered someone's great grandmaw had a cow similarly afflicted over the hills in the back country when he was a child.

"Prices' cow is bewitched." They summed it up.

"The problem at hand is how to break the spell."

"We reckon you need a charm."

To supply that need, to the store one day, came Lyin' John Singleton. Even liars have been known to tell the truth at times. He was from way down in the river hills. Way, way down, where all kinds of spells are worked.

He explained it,

"Someone is mad at you, so they put a spell on your cow."

They told Lyin' John the beginning of it.

"Old Nannie cow saw something goshawful at the old black stump. She reared and snorted and pawed the ground."

"For certain Nannie cow is bewitched."

Lyin' John turned up the sole of his shoe and began whetting his knife and squinting one eye to encourage his thinking.

"The question is two-fold. Who put on the spell? And how to break the spell? No worse luck in the world than for your milk not to churn butter. You need bad to find a witch."

Here is where the first witch comes in. There will be two.

Some very early recollections concern a mysterious ancient woman called Old Beck. Maw used to hush my crying by whispering,

"Old Beck will get you."

Native women called Old Beck's name up the bunghole of the vinegar barrel and said to each other, their mouths wry, "Old Beck's name is sure to sour the vinegar."

Old Beck was a withered ninety years. She lived in a hut in a gloomy hollow, reputed as haunted, so visitors were few. Among the hill people Old Beck was both feared and respected. She was respected because she "doctored" as a midwife over the hills and hollows; she was feared because she was supposed to possess the powers of a witch.

"Someone is mad at me. I wonder who?" Maw talked on.

"I remember the day Old Beck passed by, as I was milking. I looked up and there was Old Beck looking over the gate."

"You have a fine cow," is what she said. She had passed on looking evil enough. Nannie cow had always acted violent toward her, and this time, looked after her in deep thought.

On another occasion, Maw remembered she was washing outside in the kettle.

"I looked up and Old Beck was looking over the fence."

"I like to borrow some clabbermilk. A little blue-john to make the cheese," is what she said.

Maw knew she did not mean borrow but meant give, out and out.

"I am short on clabbermilk. I am near out myself. It is near churning time when I'll have extra."

Old Beck had looked at Maw through the palings of the fence, mumbled, and hobbled on up the hollow, looking backward toward Maw over her shoulder. She looked like the tarantula in my book as she hunched along angrily, throwing her legs outward like the legs of a spider.

"I thought at the time she did not like it about borrowing the milk. Could she be the one? My milk hasn't churned from that day."

Maw went to work in her garden. She had a habit of burying her troubles in the garden. When she hung her hoe over the palings, I could tell Maw had made up her mind for some action.

So Maw arose early the next morning, that was going to be a pretty day, for a trek over the high fields and down the other side into the hollow where Old Angerine lived.

Now enters the second witch — Old Angerine, who liked Maw. If anyone would know what to do, she would. Old Angerine was in the high fields picking blackberries and coming in home with a bucket full, her split bonnet hanging by its strings, on her arm. The blackberries were black and beautiful as they lay heaped in the bucket. The sun glinted off the blackberries and when I looked into Old Angerine's eyes there was the same black glisten, all bright, luscious, and fruity. For this reason, whenever Old Angerine looked at me, I thought,

"Blackberry eyes."

Old Angerine, this ancient old woman with her weathered face, always carried a stick, which served various purposes. In addition to supporting her weight, she hit bulls, or old buck sheep, or vile snakes. Poisonous rattlesnakes did not phase her if she had her stick.

Now, on this particular day, she had her apron rolled up around her waist, for she had gathered herbs like snake root, sassafras, and lobelia, the healing remedies she knew so well.

As the three of us walked downward on the trace, we came upon some golden seal growing. Old Angerine began gathering it into her apron.

"Here is some golden seal. Hold some in your mouth and chew on it. Never mind the bitter taste."

She thrust the golden seal at me and watched until I put it into my mouth. Then she thrust some at Maw.

"Good for sore throat. Good for croup, too. Take some home with you. Put it in your pocket."

We walked along and Old Angerine took her stick and began turning over rocks until she found what she was looking for. She picked up a small white egg. It was just a little smaller than a bantam egg or a bad luck hen egg. The egg looked like it had been rolled in salt. Old Angerine handed the egg to Maw, all the lights twinkling in her blackberry eyes.

"Here, put this in your pocket. Take it home to Bud. It is a snake egg. It will hatch a blacksnake."

Old Angerine's blackberry eyes glistened and she laughed to herself as we walked along. Down in the river hills you don't tell the business of your visit right at first. You talk over all the news to let the business rest until near the end of the visit.

Finally, in a quiet lapse, Old Angerine said, "How air ye all? Who is sick? Is anybody dead? Whose time has come?"

Whose time has come? This question referred to midwifery. Any witch worthy of the name could catch babies. Both Old Beck and Old Angerine were called upon by the hill people to assist at bornings. Maw got Angerine to be the midwife when I was born instead of Old Beck. There may have been more competition than I know about between the two.

So Old Angerine wondered if we had come for her to gather her necessaries into her satchel to go to the aid of some poor mother having birth pangs, agonizing with a new mouth that would have to be fed through the winters. Old Angerine mentally checked the contents of her stachel. She would need her scissors, rolls of old sheeting for bandages, rosebud salve, and various herbs.

It was strange how these new lives picked the worst weather and the late wee hours to make their grand entrance. It was stranger still to see Old Angerine come to life on these occasions. She would grab her satchel, cross footlogs in the dark after midnight, her feet in her high top shoes, dancing along. With her skirt hiked to midcalf she outdistanced anyone to the hilltops. As she topped the hill, those she outdistanced saw her, a dark silhouette against the night sky and she looked a real witch, not on a mission of mercy.

Maw took the bucket of berries and Old Angerine changed her stick to her other hand.

Maw said, "I am having the worst of luck."

"Bad luck always roostin' around. Yer kraut a spilin'? All yer hens took to crowin'?"

"My butter won't come. I believe my cow is bewitched."

"Now that could easy be. You want a remedy. I know several. I'll see can I remember the one I got from my granny when she had your trouble. It is the best one. You have insulted someone. The question, who? And for you to study it up."

"I'll try to think. I am desperate; everybody knows it. Now I couldn't even trade Old Nanny. Nobody would buy her."

Old Angerine pursed her lips, which looked brown like sticky hazel nut burrs. She looked sideways at Maw.

"Go home. Get some milk in the skillet and put it on the stove to boil. When it boils hard, stick it with a knife all over. A black cat may jump out."

With this last remark about a cat, Old Angerine cackled and looked at me and winked the blackberry lights in her eyes.

"Stick the milk several times and it will break the spell."

By this time, we had reached Old Angerine's cabin, and we sat on her porch to rest and cool off, for it was a long pull back up the hill where the trace was rocky and where, if you took one step, the briars pulled you back two.

A visitor was coming toward the porch carrying a baby wrapped in quilts. The way it was covered, the baby was sick. The mother was wanting a cure from Old Angerine but felt lucky to find Maw. Mothers were always bringing their babies for Maw to breathe into their mouths and cure them of their tisic. Maw never saw her father. He died July 17 and Maw was born November 7. So the hill people thought Maw had this power. Maw herself did not believe in this cure, but she breathed into babies' mouths anyway. When the babies got well, they said it was because Maw cured them.

This mother was thankful and went on. It would be high noon before

19

we arrived home. We left with Old Angerine walking a piece with us.

"The charm will work," she said. "No more trouble. I seen a timber rattler up by the cliff there, so look where ye be steppin'. Take this stick. Watch about crossin' over rail fences."

Going down the trace was not so tiring. I flew ahead of Maw, arms outflying like a bird. I leaped and skipped to come to full stop at a yellow moccasin flower. I would tell Bud about the moccasin flower though I suspect Bud already knew. We were honor bound to tell each other if we located moccasin flowers or lady's slippers. Bud claimed he was king of the yellow moccasin flowers. He let me be king of the pink lady's slippers. Bud said more properly I should be queen. I objected hotly to this lower rank, being already low on the numbers. Bud counted his flowers over the high ridges and he found high numbers. Though the lady's slipper was exquisite, it was rare, and I felt cheated for I could never reach a high count. I well remember when my number was eleven and Bud's count was seventy-nine. His leap in the sun was spectacular. From a high rock, to the north, the south, the east, the west, he proclaimed his glory. The echoes were pure magic.

"King — moc-ca-sin — seventy-nine — nine."

On lonely afternoons Bud's long colt legs carried him to the high knobs and ridges. His climb was straight up like a deer, never meandering, and it was impossible for me to keep up with him.

King of the yellow moccasin flowers! In all our deprivations, I was king of the pink lady's slippers. Conservation was a word not yet in our vocabulary, but we were expert in our love and care. We did not break the flowers to carry them home. We talked and looked and counted, and heeled in the earth the precious seeds. Over the yellow moccasin flowers and over the pink lady's slippers, two kings stretched their arms.

The yellow of the moccasin flower brought my thoughts to butter. How was I to return to evil, to bad luck, to knots tied by the witches in the cows' tails? Bud had pointed to the witch knots. I looked back and saw Maw coming on down the trace carrying in her head a charm to break a spell.

Next morning, Maw got her crocks emptied into the cedar churn, with brass bands and the dasher all cut out into fancy circles and pretty designs. I really admired the dasher but I did not like to churn. Neither did Bud. We wished Old Marth was not afraid of the cow and would come back. Churning was such hard work. Your arms ache; your back begins to hurt; your legs give out; your feelings hit a low; you begin to watch the clock. Finally you call for help, someone — anyone — to take over, for just a few minutes.

"It is no use, Maw. It isn't coming. The butter won't come." Bud was for giving up. There was that foam running all over, just the same.

I watched Maw get an old black iron skillet. The breakfast fire needed poking up, and a stick added. Into the skillet on top of the stove, Maw dipped some milk and we watched it heat up, steam a bit, and finally come to a rolling boil.

"What are you going to stick it with?"

Maw got the butcher knife and an old iron fork with two long prongs. Each time Maw stuck the milk with the knife or fork, the rolling boil went down. It got quiet like.

"That ought to do it."

Maw had stuck and cut vigorously. Like bloody murder. If a black cat was in there, he was stuck to death. I wanted badly to see him jump out, and I was disappointed. I raised on my toes to peep into the skillet where I expected to see the cat swimming around.

"Now we will see."

Maw's lips were firm. I was put on the churn again. How I longed for Old Marth to come back. No one was as expert as Old Marth on a churning. She knew how many long hard licks and how many short gathering licks it took. She could not count, but she knew just exactly how many licks it took to bring a ring of yellow gold around the dasher.

That morning my arms were breaking off and Bud was not cooperating. The next minute I would be crying. I doubted anything good was working. The time was so long.

I saw it. I saw it, but I did not believe it.

"Maw. I see butter. Come see if it is." Maw looked.

"The butter is coming. See the yellow specks. That is the butter. Now gather it."

Somehow I wasn't too tired. Maw's tired face straightened. I churned harder: I patted and churned and churned and patted. The dasher got heavy. It sure enough was real butter. I stuck a finger down into the yellow flakes ringed around the dasher. Yellow, just as old Nannie cow was yellow. Maw's face had an air of relief and happiness.

"The spell is broken. Old Angerine broke the spell. Our milk churns butter again."

I was the cause of Maw's face clouding up again when I asked, "Who done it? Who put the spell on old Nannie cow? Who was mad at you, Maw?"

Maw seemed to think hard as she worked the butter squeezing out the water. She salted it to taste and patted it into the butter mold. I loved the butter printer because it had a thistle flower cut into the wood which came out on the top of the butter so pretty when Maw pushed the butter out of the mold.

"What will we do now, Maw?"

"Nothing to do. All is over."

Maw wasn't going to say a name. She was pondering how to keep me from talking so much. Maw never said Old Beck's name after that. Down in the hills you never speak the name of the one who put the spell on, or your good luck charm will be broken.

"Forget it," said Maw.

But I didn't. Who? Who was the witch who put the spell? How was I to know if no one would call a name? Old Marth came back to churn and wash. While no one was looking, I entered fully my questioning period. Nannie Cow, Old Beck, Old Angerine, stored in the back of my mind, could be drawn out at any time.

Maw would give me curious looks, then look over at Old Marth. Then back at me, saying nothing.

Old Marth said, "Old Beck was the devil."

Maw nodded but called no name while Old Marth chewed on the

stem of her clay pipe. Then they both tried to change the subject to distract me. They talked about some lights Paw saw in the cedars and then how I could go to meeting next time to watch the women faint and throw their babies.

"Why did the women throw their babies?"

"What if no one caught the baby?"

"How can you get that happy?"

"What is the spirit?"

"Is everybody a witch?"

"How can I get to be a witch?"

Questions were endless. There was much talk. It made a good tale to tell up and down the hollows. How somebody put a spell on Prices' cow and how Old Angerine broke the spell. Maw kept telling me not to say anybody's name and break our good luck.

Who? Who was the witch who put the spell? Everybody knew. Everybody talked. I knew for sure and I do to this day.

It is good to know witches — *them* who can put on spells and *them* who can break spells. Witches, I knew two — Old Angerine who liked Maw, and Old Beck who did not like anybody. I sure enough saw it all happen. Old Nannie cow's milk that would not churn being stabbed with a fork to break the spell. I am proud to this day that I saw it with my own eyes, and that is why I am laying my hand on a stack of Bibles, and without crossing my fingers.

Little Jesus

When Marnie shook the dust from his feet and took the road to West-by-God-Virginia, the road had left the Hollow, and when roads change, soon the people leave, following the road. Little Jesus went away to the wars, never to return. Boy lay in the high hilltop cemetery close to heaven's bosom, and Old Meg's bones had been carted away to the sink-hole where they bleached white from the sun, until washing rains covered them deep. I left, too, city ways becoming my ways.

"Goodbye, Marnie. Maybe all the eggs in West Virginia won't be bad luck eggs."

Whose story is this? — Marnie, Boy, Old Indian Wood Chopper, Old Meg, possibly all of us. Maybe, most of all, the story belongs to Little Jesus.

"Come back, Little Jesus." I am always looking for his return. I answer a knock at my door to see if he might be standing there. Searching the faces of the hippie children in the street, I am chagrined, realizing I would not know him.

Things suddenly began to change, for boys grew up fast, and a way of life was left behind long ago and forgotten. The cabins fell into decay, the old traces grew over with red pokeberries, thistle, and milkweed, giving way to briars. Some followed the road; others stayed, to die and be buried atop the hill with Little Boy and Old Richmond Singleton, close to heaven's bosom.

With its people gone, only the Hollow remained, that sunless Hollow, full of its shadows where darkness descended long before twilight. I was one of them. One of the Hollow people. Sand from its high ridges and red sand gullies are in my bone marrow and are rubbing and scratching and fretting there.

One of those feathery mountain snows had arrived, on the warm and still December night so long ago. It covered the persimmon ridges, the outcropping rocks, the pointed hills, and the sand gullies, hiding all transgressions of nature and of men.

It was like things would be right for every creature — even for Old Clare and Little Jesus.

On that natal night, the church had the Christmas exercises, and we trudged to see Mary and the Babe. Among the animals around the improvised crêche was a real live mother sheep whose lamb had arrived early, and the lamb dozed in the straw or walked about on stiff black legs, as it pleased.

We went — Little Jesus, Marnie, Boy, and I. We were a foursome. Really, Old Meg, our mare, made us five. We went from no great religious training or intentions toward religiosity. It was a custom.

From the smallest child to the oldest man, each went expecting to receive the small bag of candy. As the Christmas season approached, the church members had chipped in coins so all could be treated to the bag of candy. Old and young attended in droves, with great expectancy, edging close to the Christmas Babe, in a box of straw. A lantern shed light over a young girl seated among the animals where the Babe was lying stiff and staring like a mummy, in the prepared box.

We stood in circles around the crêche. There came a suspended pause, when the black mouth of the ewe stopped for a moment chewing on the straw. We became a painting, like an old masterpiece. After the moment, everyone breathed again and moved away.

The lantern light suffused a soft glow over Marnie's face and filled the deep-cut twisted lines on the bad side and made it like the good side.

Outside there was a glow as light from somewhere sifted through the falling flakes of snow. My mother had supplied the lace tablecloth for Mary's headdress, and we were carrying it, folded, back home. Possibly we were slightly drunk from the beauty of the pageant and the miracle of the falling snow, for we decided to decorate Old Meg and make the old mare beautiful. We spread my mother's lace tablecloth over Old Meg's back, making a blanket.

Marnie, always quick to spot the pieces of candy of large size and pretty color, had already swapped out Little Jesus, and in good fettle at a favorable bargain, had hoisted Little Jesus up behind the three of us, on Old Meg's back. Snowflakes fell softly in the glow, over the four of us sitting on the lace table spread.

Since we carried no lantern, we depended upon Old Meg's sure foot to carry us safe and whole over every slick rock, over every frog hole, and along the narrow treacherous paths.

Little Jesus clung tenaciously as he slid about over the mare's rump. It is to our credit that we let Little Jesus cling on, that glowing night, for usually on our night excursions, we let him follow along behind, holding to Old Meg's tail. Going through creeks, we delighted and yelled and laughed to kick up Old Meg and get Little Jesus thoroughly splashed. He always clung to the mare's tail and made it to the other side, but he went home thoroughly drenched from our night journeys.

That Christmas Eve, we were full of a jingle-bell happiness so that the snowflakes were showers of stars and the world was hung with tinsel streamers. The excitement went right down into our toes, and we dug into Old Meg's side to make her step faster. Then we played a game, seeing how far over her sides we could lean, without sliding off.

A custom of the Hollow people was to attach the prefix _Old_ to names. We had little use for surnames and rarely used them. The use of this idiom did not necessarily bespeak age since it was attached to both young and old, man and animal alike — Old Indian Woodchopper, Old Crow and Marnie. The connotation came from a long-time familiarity, a long acquaintanceship among us. The use of _Old_ was not degrading. Though at times it might show a certain disrespect, oftentimes its connotation was one of camaraderie.

Old Crow, Old Clare — your surnames then were not important. To resurrect them now seems irrelevant. I am not sure if I could recall them.

"Come like Jesus."

I recall his birth. Little Jesus, I mean. A question remained un-

answered, then, as it does today. Who was the father? Old Clare carefully guarded her secret. Over and over speculations were bandied
about, but no one ever really found out.

Who was the father? He may have been closer kin to some of us than
we dreamed.

I recall Old Clare being 'laid in." The baby was heard crying, but a
denial was issued to what all the neighbors knew to be a fact. Each put
the question at his own time and in his own way. The classic answer
came when the question was put directly to Old Clare.

"Who is the daddy?"

"Got no daddy. Come like Jesus."

Blasphemy is to be doubted in this case, but the name stuck and the
baby was named Little Jesus, alternating sometimes with Second Jesus.

Old Clare kept her secret well. She never married. She was unlike
Old Lil who padded her stomach and *said* she was going to have a baby
to get old, idiotic, and simple Noah to the Old Square's house where the
Old Square lay abed so ill and old and rheumy he could no longer remember the words of the marriage ceremony. He stumbled and forgot
and called to his wife who couldn't remember them either.

"No difference, you are married anyway."

This may be Little Jesus' story. It was he who gave us our laughs,
and made us feel superior. He served our purposes well, and if we per-
secuted him, children bear few guilt complexes. He bore the brunt of
our cruel jokes; when worse came to worst, and we got caught at something, we could "pack it off" on Little Jesus just by looking in his direction, the same as pointing a finger. He took the accusing glances and
the blame never saying a word, for when a boy has no father to look out
for him and take his part, lots of blame falls in his direction, and it is
usually best if he stands mute.

I listen but I can draw nothing up from memory. Not one word he
ever said comes back. I try to hear his promise to return, but the vague
words seem to be my own. Things suddenly began to change. We grew
up fast. Little Jesus was gone.

"To the army someplace," they said.

He never came back. Just a card came to a neighbor after the years, asking, "How are they all?"

I don't think anyone ever bothered to answer, since literacy was scarce among the Hollow people. Old Clare could not read and write, but knew about the card.

"How are the old folks?" I fancy Little Jesus might ask.

"Well," I would tell him, "Well."

I went to the funeral parlor to see Old Clare. I knew of her passing from the obituary column in the small city where I lived. I heard that she had suffered from a malignancy, so I went expecting to see one emaciated from disease and eighty-odd years of life. I wanted to go. It was a mixture of curiosity and that other thing. If Little Jesus ever came back, I could tell him that I saw her.

Again it was the Christmas season and I could hardly spare the time to drive through the snow to the chapel. The carpet on the floor was as soft as those remembered snowflakes. No one was in attendance because it was suppertime. The atmosphere of the room was permeated by a soft glow, caused, I suppose, by the pink lights used by modern undertakers. I approached the casket breathless, and for the moment suspended breathing.

These similar moments between earth and eternity can be witnessed in hospitals, just after visitors' hours, when the lights are dimmed and the priest has passed through leaving his literature. The earth pauses, the babies in the birth canal are still, all pain stops, the elevators are silent, moans and coughs of the patients subside. Just in that moment, everything is suspended for that something which is taking place.

So I approached Old Clare for a quick look, intending to hurry away.

Old Clare was not as I expected, but fair and young-looking with an aura of blondness and of youth. The disease had taken no toll, nor had the years.

I had never seen the living people of that sunless hollow clean, never dressed in a suit, yet in that final viewing, they lay clean and young-looking. Though I was familiar with the undertaker's makeup and intravenous fluids, I was unprepared to see Old Clare lying fair and chaste, as lilies in the snow.

Come like Jesus.

"Old Clare, your lips are sealed. Keep your secret."

There was not a hint of a transgression in that rather holy chapel, with its rose of sharon light. Whose transgression? Maybe no one's. Maybe that's just the way it was for Old Clare and for Little Jesus.

I left without seeing anyone and was glad.

Little Jesus served our purposes well. He drove in the cows from the highest points; he recovered our balls from the dew-wet grass and never whimpered when his cracked bare feet got dew poisoned; he fetched the mountain tea from the distant ridges; at our bidding, he went to the hazelnut bushes high on the persimmon ridges and brought nuts down and placed them in our hands; he climbed to the top of bending birches and delivered the tenderest tips for us to chew.

"Taste the ewe sheep's milk," we told him.

Marnie said, "The milk tastes bitter. Just like the old sheep's wool smells."

For the sake of cleanliness, my father cut off the sheep's tails. It was my job to hold the sheep's tail against the chopping block as Father wielded the axe. One heavy blow by the axe and I was holding a sheep's tail in my hands. This was a loathsome job, and Little Jesus would stand in my place for some tidbit — mountain tea, or a bit of biscuit, or a handful of black haws.

Surely Little Jesus ran our errands and stood in our places more to keep our continuing friendship than for the handful of black haws. For after hanging on the bush all winter, the haws were hard and dried, and Little Jesus would have to hold them in his mouth a long while before they became succulent.

We hunted wild bees in the banks and let Little Jesus poke them out with a long stick. When we heard the angry drone coming for us, we

ducked and let the long black line pass over our heads. We issued Little
Jesus no warning and meant him to get stung. Stung he always was, for
it was sometime before he learned to duck. Meantime, we got our fun as
the seasons changed into years.

Getting apples out of the hole, in deep winter, one had to put an arm
back in the hole after removing boards and dirt. Just before the apples
was a layer of straw, in which field mice, finding a warm place, often
holed up for the winter. It was Little Jesus' job to push his hand
through the straw, so if there were field mice to run out, they would run
up his britches leg. Then we would strip him down with the excuse of
shaking the field mice out. I supposed we lacked education — sex education, in current mode. We exposed his stark white nakedness, and the
white childishness of him gleamed and resembled the frost and white
patches of snow around the apple hole.

"Pricked to die," he stood before us in white nakedness. I looked
away up the hill to where my indian pipes were wont to stand, thinking
they must be witnessing our ritual. The indian pipes were mine. It was
one of the games we played. We claimed flowers as we claimed trees.
The Judas tree, a service, a golden catalpa, a red beauty of a maple, we
owned them all. We found early spring flowers blooming, in wild se-
cluded spots, far up some cove, near a spring seep. The adder's-tongues
belonged to Marnie. The indian pipes were mine, for I had discovered
them by an old rotting log.

Now, Little Jesus seemed akin to the indian pipes with their strange
eeriness, like from some faraway time and place, and with their fra-
gility. The winter was not the time of indian pipes. Little Jesus submit-
ted to our raising his britches, and then we each reached in the hole and
got an apple to eat.

As winter receded and spring returned, we let Little Jesus try out the
pools of water to see how cold the water was. He always swam naked
two weeks before the rest of us. We let him pick up the blacksnakes,
bats, or an old sow's pigs. Once an especially ill-natured ground hog

nailed him in the hand, and he lifted his hand high with the ground hog holding on to the flesh and the blood streams trickling down his arm, causing us to retch and be sick at our stomachs.

There were chimney sweeps, phoebes, and swallows, all full of bird lice. Every bird's nest near the rafters of the old house, caked by mud daubers, was full of millions of bird lice. The birds fell down the chimney and could not get out. We caught them flapping at glass-paned windows and tied ribbons and strings to their tails.

"Jesus birds," we called them.

And every bird flying over those immediate hills had a string or ribbon flying from its tail.

"Jesus birds," we called them, because at first we did not dare own up to the secret meetings in that old abandoned house, where the birds fell down the chimney, and we let Little Jesus catch and hold them so he would get the lice, while we stripped an old apron into strings and tied the strings to the birds' tails.

Little Jesus took the lice as he took the blame, glad to travel in our company.

Marnie, older and wiser than we were, taught Little Jesus' baby mouth his choicest foul words, delighting when Little Jesus would repeat them, on most inappropriate occasions, like before Old Preacher, or before the Old Woman who Lived with a Goose.

Marnie had already watched through the cracks of planks when Old Lide and Old John went to milk the cows at night and stayed too long. Incest was not in Marnie's vocabulary, but he had a word for it. Though he taught Little Jesus the word, I am sure he never, in any way, violated Little Jesus.

"Damn these old dewberry briars," Little Jesus said.

They were carrying Old Belve to the highest hill where they buried. The top of the highest hill was closest to heaven. It was hard, slippery work as men carried the wooden box my father had made to size, by a measuring stick. The body of the corpse was measured by a reed; my father made the pine box to fit. Over the ceiling of our house were many different lengths, and Father could name whose reed it was, for Father had followed, for a long time, the practice of coffinmaker. My father, the Old Square, fashioned the planks and rubbed them down with care, keeping a bolt of cheap black cloth to cover the boards. When he wanted to do an especially fine job, he would drape the cloth along the sides of the coffin box. In no finer style could anyone desire to be put away, than in one of Father's boxes. Many black boxes had been carried up the hill to rest close to heaven's bosom, near the resting place of Old Richmond Singleton.

Footing was insecure, and loosened rocks made climbing the hill slow. Behind followed the family and neighbors. Little Jesus ran ahead of the body, which was contrary, and a man ordered him back behind. Dewberry briars have mean stickers especially on bare legs, and the scratches bring blood that runs and dries into black cakes.

"Damn to hell these old dewberry vines."

Little Jesus called out some of Marnie's choice words, in all that quietness, solemnity, trudging, and pulling that would get Old Belve to his final resting place. Marnie considered it the highlight of the whole funeral and was in high relish since he had taught Little Jesus those words that desecrated the funereal air.

"That Little Jesus will come to a bad end," was forecast up and down the Hollows.

The graveyard was overrun with briars and fallen sandrocks. The stone of one Richmond Singleton stood out larger than any other. A grand name, pointing to some grander place and lineage, but resting in the lost cemetery.

Here among the graves marked by fallen sandstones, we all had scampered and played. Here after climbing the tall hill we had urinated. Marnie and Little Jesus had filled with foam and sputters the cracks of

all that was left of the carvings of the grand sounding words RICH-
MOND SINGLETON.

We were not made for tears.

Once at school a boy asked Little Jesus that question. "Who is your
daddy?"

Little Jesus sat outside on the steps after the bell until the teacher
went out and led him in to his seat. If anyone stayed in on geography, it
was he, which, I am now sure, he did not mind. After everyone had
gone ahead, Little Jesus could search the ditches along the road for
apple cores, bits of biscuits, or other discarded items from the dinner
pails of the scholars going home. These were the old days before school
lunches.

When Marnie stuck his toes in the dust and went off down the road to
West-by-God-Virginia, he left his wise old face which has looked back
across the intervening years, ever young, forever old.

Marnie had watched the bulls in the pasture. He was old enough to
aid a neighbor who had to drive a cow for breeding. Marnie looked
with sharp eyes and reported back to us. He hoped Little Jesus would
use some of the knowledgeable words in the church house. Marnie
liked to watch the looks on faces; he was a watcher. On one side of his
face he carried the eternal, wise sneer.

He had listened to the old folks in their beds while he pretended
sleep in his. He was "the liar." Once while visiting his apple tree for
late-hanging apples, he had followed a hunter over the hills, hypnotized
by his gun. He had watched while the hunter bore to the ground with a
piggy-back clutch a girl already known to be plying her trade when she
was ten years old.

Marnie watched.

"Go, or you will get killed," the hunter said. They rolled off in the
sage grass.

Marnie went screaming and told.

"Liar" he was made out to be, and he did not deny it when he registered the girl looking little the worse for her tumble.

But Marnie knew, and on his face he kept the half-sniggering sneer. He was wised up. He tried to wise us up, and told Little Jesus some words to use.

Brush arbors would be set up as itinerant preachers came through the Hollow. For some technical reason, these servants of God were denied holding services in the church house. So brush arbors for their accommodation were constructed on some brushy-wooded side of a hill. The underbrush was cleared away, trees felled for seats, and an improvised altar set up.

Old intrigues would be renewed and new ones initiated. Many sought the "angel food" as the preacher exhorted, and his bunch of exhorters got confessions and reinstatements.

The preachers generally were hellfire preachers. Marnie sat in the back where he could watch, watch who sat behind whom, who whispered over shoulders, who winked at whom, or who left early to join in a love tryst.

At our own little meeting, Marnie would tell Little Jesus, "I can smell them burning in hellfire."

And he began to name names, and smirked on one side of his face.

"They smell like old burnt meat." Marnie could always spot a son of a bitch, and sometimes he would pronounce a blanket opinion.

"They are all sons of bitches."

Marnie had a bearskin coat. It was a child's coat and homemade. The color was blonde, and it was hard for me to imagine the tawny bear whose coat it once was, for the bear in my reading book was black. The coat was too small for Marnie and no longer fit him. Others tried to get it away from him but could not. He used it in very cold spells to wrap his knees or spread over his feet at night. The coat always hung on a wooden peg by the door. I would have liked to own it.

o   o   o

In summer the snake meetings were held out of doors. Down on the lower end of the Hollow was a rocky spot with plenty of rocks to rest on. The meeting spot was located far from the side of the Hollow used for brush arbors because snake handlers did not associate with brush-arbor preachers.

Lots of folks just visited and saw old friends. They made the yearly trip down from high ridges and out of the numerous coves. Old ladies had carefully preserved their ancient hats and long black skirts in boxes by wrapping them in layers of paper. Year after year, they came wearing them down the ridges, looking for old friends who got fewer each year.

It was an all-day meet. Each brought a basket of food, and friends would get together and spread dinner on the ground.

Rattlesnakes and copperheads were plentiful on the sand ridges and not too hard to catch with a forked stick. One did not have to keep them boxed separately, since the snakes lived together in their dens.

These particular snakes were brought in from Saint Paul by some Brothers who were repaying a visit. The preachers supported each other in their various meets by visiting and helping one another.

The preachers unloaded the snakes out of their old black hack. The snakes were all tied up in boxes stored under the platform where the Brothers stood. The Brothers kept saying they were going to bring the snakes out. This went on all day long, and it was a ruse to keep the crowd from leaving.

Old Preacher and Old Rowe worked the crowd diligently begging for a love offering, which was a collection for the Saint Paul Brothers. Old Preacher knew he would not get the offering this time, but when he went to repay the visit, to help in the Saint Paul meet, all the money given to the Lord would be his to bring back home to the Hollow. So Old Preacher worked the crowd with vim.

Bootleggers lounged on the outer fringe of the gathering and could be seen taking walks up in the woods where homebrew was hidden, buried under the leaves.

"I am an angel of the Lord, come down to drink up all the whiskey, so the other people won't drink it."

This old drunk wore a sponge soaked in spirits on top of his bald head under his old hat so that his brain could get the effects of the whiskey quicker. It was something about his insides having scars and deposits, like an old teakettle.

"Bring out the snake."

It took a long time, about four hours, to get the crowd worked up and worked out of cash, the Brothers foaming in a frenzy.

"Let those who have the faith to take the test come forward."

A Sister strummed on the dulcimer, loud and inviting. I felt I would like to take a test, for I believed. I loved God. I wanted to join that group that moved forward, hands reaching heavenward, whose human hearts were awakened to love and desire to undergo the test. Marnie kept his big foot firmly down hard on top of my foot.

"If you get bitten, you just don't have enough faith," the Brother said.

The Brother reaches under the platform and brings out a box. He unties the box, but holds down the lid with one hand.

"Amen," he calls. In darts a hand and he holds high in the air a black copperhead, which seems dazed as it wriggles trying to find a solid footing and finally wrapping its tail around the Brother's arm. The old snake sways to the woman's music. As it sways it seems to keep good time with an ugly head darting left and right.

The Brother doesn't hold the snake overlong, but flings it out into the crowd whose upreaching hands pitch the snake quickly about among themselves. You really have to be alert, for the snake is likely to be tossed your way. Like a hot potato, get rid of it. The snake is tossed about like a tip ball until he finally reaches the other end where someone whams him back into his box. The Brother assists by shutting down the lid quickly. It is breathtaking. The Brother wipes the sweat from his face.

I recall one old rattlesnake who got loose out of his box. There was consternation as the Brothers shook their britches and turned around and about like tops. The old woman in the black hat shrieked, and mothers stood their children up on high rocks. Skirts and petticoats were lifted and ankles revealed in a time when it was sinful to show your leg. Lots of swains got choice looks and tidbits, to later enlarge upon, forgetting to look for the snake. By this time, the old woman in the black hat was poised high on a higher rock. On tiptoe, in her high topped button shoes, she seemed ready to take flight. Her hat shed pieces of feathers and moth dust that sifted downward.

Some boys saw the snake sliding among some loose rocks where he disappeared.

This broke up the meeting. Old Preacher had been looking right through the pearly gates with his face lifted toward heaven. Now he was yelling.

"Get a shovel. Dig him out. Where is a forked stick to hold him down? Marnie, come get him."

"Nothing doing. I'm barefooted." That was Marnie.

Meanwhile the dogs ran yipping about, the hackles raised on their necks. For a snake to get away and breed a season would not be good for future meetings. The people would remember and not come.

Truly, the snake was among us. Upsetting. Where was he? People looked under their feet, to finally look closely in each other's eyes. Everybody knew the pupils of the eyes of a poisonous snake stand straight up. They believed they saw the snake peering out of each other's eyes. They peered and imagined they saw things. A cold wind began to blow down off the ridges, and the people thought of getting home.

"Some here could mate with the old rattlesnake, they so mean." Marnie jumped high and cracked his heels together three times.

I began to feel like it was one of the best of times.

"We'll go down one of these days and dig around. I saw where he went. Let's hightail it for home," Marnie said.

The Saint Paul Brothers got real mad. I saw them pack their boxes back in their old hack to leave, shoving the woman with the dulcimer around roughly.

All the folks scattered quickly on the ridge traces, going homeward into the distant coves. Some were already so far ahead that they seemed to be barely moving, like cattle or wagon trains, or buffaloes, on the trail. At the far distances, they were unreal miniatures, toylike.

Boy lived with Old Indian Wood Chopper and his Indian wife, Old Crow. Boy was a nonentity. He was like a girl with uncut hair, wearing overall castoffs and a sort of oversize shirt. As I said, he did not count for much. We saw his old pads hung on the line to dry on fair days. We knew by the brown circles that he still wet his bed. Nobody had ever bothered to name him, but a Sunday School teacher fixed it real nice for Boy.

"Boy. Oh, no. It is Boyd," and she wrote it down for him.

Old Crow's cough medicine did not seem to help much his turnip complexion, all white with purplish lips. We tolerated him, but he did not count for as much, even, as the sleep-tears in the corners of his eyes. I never remember seeing Boy without the sleep-tears in his eyes.

If Old Crow saw anyone approaching, she would go back inside her house. I know of no living soul she ever spoke to. She went back and forth to a tiny garden, carrying things in her lap.

Her scarecrow for the birds frightened both birds and boys. She trapped the crows that bothered her garden corn, and on a long pole she hung a dead one, terrible to see, where it flapped and swung to frighten away other crows. This is why we called her Old Crow. I was scared of her but Boy and Marnie were not, for they both had lived with her in other, harder times.

She buried things like cabbage heads in her garden, and left the roots sticking high in the air. Her herbs, like shawnee and mullein root and heartweed, were tied in little bundles and hung to dry high along the porch rafters.

She could brew a powerful and respected cough syrup from mullein roots, which Old Indian Wood Chopper carried around in bottles, in his pockets, for sale.

Through the paling fence, we watched Old Crow smoke a pipe with a long reed stem and a clay bowl, into which she put a mixture of corn silks, old dried moss, and rabbit tobacco. It was grand to watch her smoke, this ancient mysterious apple-faced creature. A grander smoker I have never seen, as she drew the smoke through the reed to come out the other side of her mouth in little contented puffs.

Once she grew a crop of great yellow squashes and kept them piled high on her porch until the freezes came. She piled her squashes on the porch where passersby could view her fine crop. It was a one-man show. The round golden squashes, like a woman's breasts, were voluptuous and luscious, like the udders of a freshened cow. There were white squashes and green striped ones with crooked necks, and one as huge as a tub.

The green stripes on the crook necks were the same green stripes of the snake we watched up near some rocks at the spring seep. He or his progeny crawled out each year when warm suns hit the rocks and he got the message. Once we had rocks poised to break his body and bash his head, but Marnie said, "No." The snake was his. We watched while the snake slithered among the adder's-tongues, which Marnie claimed also. The green yellow stripes of the snake mixed with the sun spots on the leaves of the adder's tongues, where Nature received and claimed the snake as her own. It would be hard now to find the snake, covered by last year's brown matted leaves.

Above the squashes, Old Crow strung her gourds to the high rafters of her porch. Marnie had a gourd made into a birdhouse and it was hanging in a tree near his cabin. Little Jesus would have liked one of the gourds, too. So we asked Marnie, "Couldn't you get us one?"

Marnie said, "No," though he had ways of appropriating things for himself — by swapping, trading, maybe otherwise.

We watched through the paling fence of the garden until Old Crow came and stood, flapping her apron, frightening boys and birds into a giddy scatterment.

Old Indian Wood Chopper made boards with a beetle mallet and a froe. He knew just the right season to make boards so they would not curl up toward the sun on the cabin roofs.

We came upon his various work sites in the woods. Here would be a stack of shingles neatly stacked; there, a pile of rotting chips and splinters and shavings.

In early morning, the echo of woodchopping came from the ridges and resounded up and down the Hollow.

Over all those years, Old Indian Wood Chopper bothered no one. He was harmless. Something inscrutable, elemental, with a wildness near to the forest, was in Old Indian Wood Chopper's eyes. As we skylarked over the ridges for all those years, I am sure we were watched from behind trees and from hilltops. I doubt that we were ever alone. Out in the big world, my guardian angel did not have two black chinquapin eyes. Even later, at a school far away, I tried in a science book to find the life cycle and scientific name, but these escaped me. Old Indian Wood Chopper knew many of the answers, but disclosing them was contrary to his nature.

We hung over a paling fence to watch the Old Woman Who Lived with a Goose pick the breast feathers from it, joining hilariously in the commotion of feathers and squawks.

Little Jesus was chosen to hold down the goose, and he would get the fuzz up his nostrils, and the old goose would bite him good before he clamped her mouth closed, holding her bill together with his fingers.

The feather-picking squawks may be compared to a hog slaughtering, where the hogs catch on, and grunts and squeals spell out tragedy in the pig world. Marnie said, "It don't hurt Old Goose if you know how to jerk the feathers out quick." I don't know if it hurt the old goose to pluck her breast feathers or not, but she objected terribly to this feather-picking operation.

Old Woman gave Little Jesus a bad-luck egg, which we did not know was a bad-luck egg until later.

I do not know what trade Marnie contracted with Little Jesus, but Marnie got the egg and carried it around in his pocket until it began to shake watery sounds inside.

Marnie got afraid the egg might break and put rottenness in his pocket. So we decided to bury the egg between the roots of the old oak tree, where we covered it with green moss.

We looked sometime later and the black ants had taken over. So we knew the egg had been rotten a long, long time before coming into our hands.

We had passed by the house of the Old Woman Who Lived with a Goose several times and saw no one. We often visited her and we were in a stopping mood.

"Let's stop and hear her talk."

Marnie rapped on her door until she called, "Come in."

She was sick in bed so she was right glad to see us this time. She was in bed under the feather ticks, and she might have been the goose herself, with her white hair and black eyes looking at us out from under the feathers.

"We thought you was the goose." Marnie spoke my thoughts.

"If you unzes want che unz a chair, go and get che unz one."

Her dialect was from some other place, and her way of talking was different. But we understood her all right. We liked to hear her talk, and asked her questions.

"You always been here? Where did you used to live?"

"I was born in Carter County. I used to know where it is, but I don't know where it is any more. I forget where Carter County is."

"What time is it?"

"What time air it? You think I can't tell you what time it air. But I can done it." Old Woman squinted toward the window and the sun. She had unique ways of telling time. Like the space of an hour she measured rather accurately as the time it took her to make a fire and get a kettle of water boiling.

"Have you seen Old Bull?" Marnie tantalized her. He had asked Old Woman this question before, so he already knew what she would say, for Old Woman had refined moods in her ways of talking.

"You mean gentleman cow. No, I ain't seen him in a spell."

"Gentleman cow, hell," Marnie would say later. "A bull is a bull."

"Why do you keep your feet sticking out from under the covers?" We could see the long white legs of her ordered winter underwear, and her feet with her little boots on.

"My old feet. Nothing to do 'em any good. No doctor medicine. Nothing but putting 'em out from under the kiver and getting 'em cold. Then I put 'em back under the kiver and they begin to warm up and begin to feel better."

"I can order from Roebuck, too." This came after a silence.

We could tell this from her room, for the walls were all papered with catalogue leaves. We liked to look around in her pretty room. Her whole house was the cleanest place, smelling so fresh and good. She had crocheted lace medallions that hung from the fireplace mantel, which looked, for the world, like giant snow flakes.

She had a crazy quilt, as she called it, for her bed, and it was made of thousands of tiny pieces all sewed together with a stitch that looked like a rail fence. She stood her pillows up tall and covered them with pillow shams. These were lacy and ruffled and one said "Good Night" and the other had "Good Morning" embroidered on it. Now the crazy quilt and pillow shams were neatly folded across the head of Old Woman's bed.

We sat gingerly on Old Woman's chairs, for one time she had run us off. Somebody had put a handful of chinches, mashed chinches, on top of her hot stove. They began to heat up and it was something awful. There is no worse scent in this world than crushed chinches burning.

Marnie denied doing this, but we had had to leave quickly.

Old Woman always watched us after this. We could sit on her chairs, but she did not permit us to move about in her house.

Old Woman did not want chinches in her bed and walls, papered so pretty with leaves from the Roebuck catalogue.

We watched her when she went visiting or to the church house. Outside her house, before opening her door, she would take off her voluminous petticoats and go around the tucks and hems on the bottoms looking for chinches.

"Looking for chinches," said Marnie. "I don't blame her. One time I stayed in this house all night. The sons-of-bitch chinches played ball games on the wall all night. Chinches don't like light, so just light the lamp and they will go back in the walls and hide. Just light the lamp and the sons-of-bitches won't bite you all night. You have to know what to do."

Old Woman talked to herself. She may have forgotten us sitting there, for her next speech became lengthy.

"My fire took off good in my little stove. I had a fine meal. The beans I grew in my garden last summer. A neighbor brought me a bowl of beans, and I laughed, for now I'll have two kinds of beans. I made some cornbread and ate some canned tomatoes. I tended the tomatoes growing on their vines. The pickles, I made myself. So I have lots to think about. I just warm myself and sit a while in my chair. Then I go to my good bed. Feathers underneath and feathers above. There I'll keep warm all the night. I might not wake up, so I'll ask God to take me home to heaven to be with him — me and the goose."

This rambling was becoming monotonous, so Marnie broke into her thoughts.

"Who do you say you talk to?"

"Why, God and the goose. If I want to know anything, I talk to the goose."

"Would you steal?"

This riled Old Woman and changed her mood. "I don't steal. I do not steal. I would ask them for some peaches. Maybe they would give me some. I'd like to have some nice peaches."

Then Old Woman offered us some parsnips to take home. She grew real fine parsnips in her garden and was always offering to give parsnips to somebody.

Marnie refused the parsnips and told us later, "Parsnips are the next thing to c'yarn," which was his way of saying carrion.

Old Goose was asleep in one corner under a little table. She was in a little box with her head under her wing. Marnie wanted to stir her up to walk around.

"Is your goose a boy or a girl?"

"I wouldn't have a goose that didn't lay eggs."

"How can a goose lay eggs without no gander?"

This really stumped Old Woman into thinking considerable. At the mention of her name Old Goose waddled out of her box toward Old Woman. Marnie reached out toward the goose and she hissed and bit at his finger, stretching out a long neck. Her feed and water pan were by the door, for when one gave her a drink you had to open the door and let her out quick.

Marnie explained the goose's anatomy, "It is like they have a straight gut. If water goes in one end, it comes right out the other end. So you better be quick."

Old Goose stood up and spread her wings, so Old Woman said, "Let her out to view the weather." To get her back in the house, all Old Woman had to do was beat on her feeding pan.

Then Old Woman had the thought we might soon be leaving, and she began to list chores for us.

Old Preacher always ate meals up and down the Hollow. Marnie questioned his religion when he would leave his wife and younguns at home by themselves in winter to gather their own firewood, and with nothing to eat.

I never knew if it was spitefulness of the Old Woman Who Lived with a Goose when Old Preacher stopped at her cabin door right at dinner time, and she cut him down some greens with the mowing scythe and threw them in a big black kettle of boiling water to cook. The iron kettle stood outside on a spider over the fire. I have often wondered if the Old Woman was fixing to wash and cooked the greens in the wash water. Anyway, it was a meal of greens and nothing else, which was good enough for Old Preacher and his sidekick, Old Rowe.

Old Preacher was supposed to brag on the meal, talk over the news, and have prayer before he left.

Most of the time Old Preacher was accompanied by Old Rowe, long of leg, of neck, of nose, of gut, and of windy prayers. They made extra visits during butchering season, when they expected to be fed tenderloin.

"Two of a kind," said Marnie. Everybody knew Old Rowe had beat his horse to death. He tied a slipknot around the horse's neck and beat him until he choked him down on the ground. With every lick of the stick the horse tried to back off, and the knot got tighter and tighter until it cut off his wind. This frightened the horse more, and, finally, when he was down on the ground, Old Rowe beat him to death as he choked.

"Old Rowe didn't pray that night." Some of his family reported this.

"I wonder why," sneered Marnie. "Old long-gutted hypocrite, with his long gut and windy prayers, don't mean nothing. Just like some cussin', some praying don't go very high or amount to much."

Old Woman's cat dressed out to be a very good rabbit. After skinning — cut off the tail, cut off the feet and head, and one can't tell a cat from a rabbit. No telling how many cats Old Preacher ate up and down that hollow.

Marnie said, "I just feel sorry for the cats."

Old Preacher knew who cooked good groundhogs. A fat hind leg of a young groundhog had to be soaked over night in salt water, boiled down with an onion, stuck with spicewood toothpicks, and baked with sweet potatoes. Now that was real eating. In the fall of the year, groundhogs grew fat on pawpaws and wild grapes. There is no food on earth with that special flavor of pawpaws and wild grapes. If you haven't tasted it in fifty years, you can still remember that flavor of a young groundhog served with sweet potatoes.

Old Preacher and Old Rowe "asseled" about up and down the Hollow. Old Rowe backed up Old Preacher; if Old Preacher said the world was coming to an end, Old Rowe said it was so. Toady that he was. They both would take anything you had right out of your pockets, like apples, chestnuts, your birch and sassafras sticks in the spring, your chinquapins in the fall, and in the winter your lard cracklings.

"Gathering chinquapins is hard work climbing over high ridges and picking them out of their burrs. People get mighty tired of those two taking things out of pockets," Marnie said.

Marnie fixed them one time when he had on his britches that had the pocket worn out. The pocket has no bottom in it anymore. When Old Preacher ran his hand in Marnie's pocket, he frowned up terrible, and I don't think he liked what he got a hold of.

Marnie said, "That fly blow," meaning Old Preacher "has taken the last chinquapin he is ever going to take off me."

So we wondered why Marnie brushed close against Old Preacher whenever they met and displayed prominently a bulging front pocket. He even held his hand over his pocket protecting it like, and drawing attention to it. Old Preacher still wasn't against running his hand into a pocket when he got the chance and helping himself.

Now on this particular morning Old Preacher and Old Rowe were almost upon us before we knew it.

"Don't stop and talk. Keep going on." Marnie told us, but we noticed he was stopping close to Old Preacher. We could not hear what was being said, but we saw Old Preacher run his hand down into Marnie's pocket, and bring out a big handful.

By this time Marnie caught up with us.

"Sheep and rabbit turds," Marnie said out of the corner of his mouth.

Sheep manure is in small round balls. So are rabbit turds. Both dry into hard round balls, not at all untidy to carry in a pocket, as one would suppose.

Looking back, we saw Old Preacher shake off his hands.

"Why you boys carrying around rabbit and sheep balls? Somebody would like to know what you boys are playing around with."

"Reasons," Marnie called back to him. We were walking fast. "Keep moving," Marnie said to us.

Marnie was onto Old Preacher's schemes, but Old Preacher had plenty of tricks.

He managed to be at the shed where the men were shearing sheep. He looked to see whom the wool belonged to. Wool meant cash, and

Old Preacher wanted to know who had a little cash. In fact, cash in anyone's pocket had a fascination for Old Preacher.

Old Preacher performed at two functions, marriages and funerals. You had to have the services of a preacher at these. Old Preacher was not at all averse to marrying a twelve year old girl to some grizzled old widower. Widowers might have a dollar for the fee, where young fellows usually had only quarters.

"How much do I owe you?" the grooms invariably asked. Old Preacher pondered and pondered.

"Whatever you think she is worth." Old Preacher collected many quarters this way.

Once I saw him marry two in a sweet potato patch. It took several days to secure a marriage license from the county seat. It was a long two-day trip by foot, maybe getting a ride on a wagon, then staying overnight.

Again I saw Old Preacher marry two across a flooded creek. He just couldn't wait for that quarter. It has rained so hard the creek was in flood over the footlog and couldn't be crossed. The bride was on one side and the groom on the other.

"Let the good work not be held up," said Old Preacher.

So Old Preacher called the questions right across the creek and they answered each other that way, too. That blamed creek didn't go down for three days, for it rained and rained. The old creek really had her big britches on that time. There were some smiles I did not understand, but Old Preacher performed his duty, flood or no flood, and he got his quarter.

Old Preacher could smell a corpse a mile. He had ways of knowing. He knew who was sick in bed; he knew who passed down the Hollow to my father's house with the measuring stick for a coffin; he knew who had the cough and was taking Old Crow's remedy. He had his ways of prolonging a funeral. As long as the food kept coming in, he thought of some far away cousin who might be coming, and they ought to wait a while for him.

At the wake they sat up all night to keep the corpse company on his last earthly sojourn. Once my father and some men sang Christian hymns all night over a child burnt up in a fire.

All kinds of business went on at a wake — eating, courtships, singing. There were those who liked to sing and those who liked to eat. Courtships were begun and consummated. Some result might make its appearance after nine months when on a rainy night the midwife would catch some squawling infant.

Finally, when the food began to play out, someone brought up burying the corpse which by this time was in a state of rigor mortis with darkened face and beginning to stink and with drippings under the coffin.

The deceased could not be buried without wearing a pair of white socks.

"Go up and down and bring a pair of white socks," they said, if the deceased were not affluent enough to own a pair. It was considered an honor to supply the white socks to complete the corpse's last toilet.

Old Preacher headed the procession as they carried the remains up the steep hill where upon reaching the top, I am not one to say that Old Preacher did not perform his duty well.

"Thank you, Lord, for letting us see the light of this another day." I was impressed.

Old Preacher, for all his foibles, performed well at all funerals, as he was to do at Boy's "planting."

I looked at him with his long nose and legs, and he seemed a bond between earth and heaven. I would not look at Marnie, for his face showed the sneering side.

"Thank you, Lord for letting us see the light of this another day." Old Preacher boomed his prayer out loud and drew it out long, and he did not seem the fake Marnie made him out to be.

Hog-killing weather was cold. It had to be cold for the meat to keep.

Down the length of the Hollow real early in the morning, the smokes of early fires told who was butchering that day. One had to rise early before daybreak, to light the fire that got the water boiling. The hog was rolled over and over in a pan of boiling water — then scraped. On a frosty morning, the white smokes rose straight upward and were visible long distances, telling the news as well as if a crier had gone up and down the Hollow.

About nine o'clock when the hog was scalded, scraped white and clean, and on the pole, the guts in a large tub and the heart and liver over by themselves in a pan, the hardest work was over.

Old Preacher and Old Rowe knew the time to arrive and would certainly make their appearance at the right time. Old Preacher stood far apart from where the womenfolks would be taking off the gut lard. He said it made him sick, claiming a faint stomach.

During hog-killing weather Old Preacher and Old Rowe were going at a lively pace toward the butchering. Old Preacher had a little song he would sing, not of a religious nature, but it seemed related to the tenderloin he was wanting to sample. As he sang it his shanks clapped together and his legs jerked knee high like a square dance.

> "Old dog standing at the gate
> Smell the meat frying
> And swear he can't wait.
> Old horse nickered
> Old cow pranced
> Old sow whistled
> And the little pigs danced."

Old Rowe stepped along behind as the wind flapped at his britches over his knees not yet used to the winter cold. Tenderloin and sausage meat. The odor went up and down the Hollow like the odor from a city bakery or from old country ham frying.

Once Old Preacher pretended it was raining, as an excuse for stopping at the sausage grinding. "It's snizzling outside. Guess I'll go shack up." Guess he was thinking how he'd snack up. That's what he stopped for — to snack up on tenderloin and sausage.

"Yonder come a man with a sack on his back." There was a little joke in the song. For a long time the meaning was lost upon us. Until Marnie explained how some son-of-a-bitch husband had stolen the best ham to give to some fancy lady. When the wife found it missing, she knew who had taken the meat, but pride closed her lips and a stoicism steeled her body to bear. She could do without the meat and a husband.

Old Preacher was great for stirring up gatherings. Corn shuckings were fun in the fall with the piled corn and the men pulling the shucks off fast and throwing the corn around.

But Old Preacher especially liked box suppers. He knew the best cooks, of course, and made sure he got to eat with the best one. Pretending to be making himself helpful, he planted himself where the boxes came in to be stacked. He received in his hands each box and could almost tell by the weight what each contained. He had a sly way of slipping back under the bench, out of sight, out of reach, the box he chose for himself.

Marnie had laughed all week. He owned some green string and Christmas paper which he had kept for a long time, so we were surprised when he brought it up on the ridge where we unrolled it and looked at it and admired it a lot.

Marnie began to tie little green love knots, like bows, out of the string. He made about a dozen little green bow knots. As he cut and tied the knots, sitting on the ground, he laughed to himself.

The box suppers generally were held on Friday nights during hog killing time. We all had gathered and were watching the boxes come in and be stacked by Old Preacher on some benches.

With my own eyes, but I pretended not to see, I saw Old Preacher take in his hands a box, covered with red Christmas paper and tied all over with green love knots. It was Marnie's box all right.

Old Preacher tested its weight, up and down, and it appeared real heavy. Like, maybe, tenderloin and biscuits. Then I saw him gingerly lay it to one side, and slyly, after a while, slide it under the bench.

I knew what was on his mind. What I didn't know was how Marnie managed to get it mixed among the other boxes without Old Preacher seeing.

Maybe Old Crow had given Marnie something for his box, which appeared to weigh good and heavy?

It was a jolly high time to see who purchased whose box, who got matched up, or who ate with whom. Everybody sat around, at first, embarrassedlike and shy.

Old Preacher never was shy. He couldn't wait to eat, as he claimed the red box with the green string for his, pretending to find it last after everybody was teamed up. He began opening her up. Off came the red paper, but the love knots slowed him down some.

This time Old Preacher was not embarrassed, he was plain mad. His mouth fell open. He was flabbergasted. He stood struck paralyzed like he was going to have a fit. Someone had really put it on him.

The pig's tail, pig's ears, pig's feet, even a pig's bladder, he could not hide. Several rocks gave some added weight. Everyone was tickled and looked at each other and guffaws burst out loud.

Old Preacher tried to cram the box back down under the bench and held up his hand for the blessing.

"We thank thee, Lord, for the light of this another day."

It was nighttime. Eight or nine o'clock. Old Preacher was right shook up.

I looked over at Marnie and he was sniggering, and we all got to giggling and couldn't stop, until we thought Old Preacher got to look-ing over our way. Then Marnie signaled for us all to move outside.

Just mention a box supper a year after that and Marnie would get tickled all over again. As we all did, thinking of a pig's tail, pig's ears, and an old pig's bladder. Even if Marnie did have to sacrifice his red Christmas paper and green string.

We did not see Marnie for days. They said he had the toothache. They said the tooth was bealing. We went to the old meeting spots, up under the hickory tree and on to the crane's nest above the spring seep. No

Marnie. We caught glimpses of him walking over the high ridges. He did not sleep at night, but sometimes by day we could see him walking.

"Have the tooth pulled," they said.

The blacksmith shop was far down the Hollow, and was partly a dugout back in a hill with the shed part built out in front. The shop was near Blue Mountain, which was not blue when you got close to it, but Big Mountain loomed blue and large behind it, and the bend in the road disappeared into the mountain leading somewhere into West Virginia. So they said.

The blacksmith was a huge man. I mean, really large. I have seen him hold an unruly horse for its first shoeing with that big arm around the horse's leg. Before the horse got away, in a matter of minutes, a shoe was on his foot. Blackie had such skill. A man who could shoe a horse was truly an artisan as he trimmed the hoof, pared off the broken split parts, cleaned out the frog, fitted and nailed on the shoe. Blackie knew just where to put the nails, not too high in the tender spots. Then with the nippers, he would nip off the nails to make a really elegant job.

Blackie had a pair of forceps which always lay back in the shop on the high shelf. They were twelve-inch forceps. Everyone knew what they were for. All hoped never to have them used in their mouths.

When you have the toothache, you stand it for a while hoping it will go away. The ache seems to get worse at night. You try all the remedies — a heated iron, laying on of the camphor, but nothing helps. You walk the floor at night and when day comes you take to the high fields trying to make up your mind. A bealed tooth takes about three days of continual pain and throbbing until you go out of your head, not caring whether you live or die. The tooth makes up your mind, and you find yourself down at Blackie's.

You don't have to say anthing. Blackie doesn't either. He just disappears back in the shop and you drop down on a round wooden block, from a great tree.

Marnie closes his eyes against the formidable forceps as Blackie comes back working them and snapping them together, testing them.

"This will be over in a minute, Marnie Boy," says Blackie, as he puts a huge arm around Marnie's head, like a giant's vise, and takes the upper jaw well in hand.

Like lightening tearing through a giant oak, like the sinews bursting the head from a giant's shoulders, the pressure from the bealing throws the pus in several directions.

As Marnie screams, Blackie gives a whoop to counteract Marnie's yell.

Blackie's great arm releases its grip. "Gallons of poison," he says.

The relief is then and there. It overtakes Marnie, as he gets so relaxed he sits resting in a stupor.

We went fishing along the creek pretending a great interest in fishing, but really keeping an eye out for Marnie.

Blackie motioned us toward a bank of sage grass. We followed and found Marnie asleep with a piece of an old homemade saddle blanket Blackie had thrown over him. He did not awaken.

Later on Marnie would open his mouth and we would look at the hole the tooth came from. Blackie saved the tooth and gave it to Marnie. It was large and yellow with three roots, the fourth root being twisted around the third. Marnie rolled the tooth in a piece of cloth and carried it about in his pocket like a fetish. On occasions he brought it out, unwrapped it, and we all looked.

It was one of those rare springs. Like heavely blue morning glories, the sky shone through myriad leaves. It found us on the high ridge chasing among clumps of orange honeysuckle. A high life in a high season, as over the honeysuckle clumps we jumped high and raced. We were little horses up and down the ridge, and over an old rail fence we chased one and another breathless, until looking backward we saw Boy hanging like an old sack on the top rail. He just sank across the rails and stayed there. We lifted him down, surprised at his lightness. For there was nothing more. Just weightlessness like a bird eaten up by lice, like an old hen that had died from cholera, her feathers fooling you till you lifted her to fling her away. Nothing there but lightness, when we laid

Boy down by the rail fence among the orange honeysuckles, while the red of the hemorrhage bubbled out the corners of his mouth.

I remember thinking Old Crow's mullein remedy had not had any effect. The turnip white that was always his face was turning to turnip blue all over.

Suddenly Old Indian Wood Chopper stood at our sides and he bent down close to Boy and looked at the turnip blue face, and he quickly rose and his chinquapin eyes bore into our eyes.

"Fly! Tell somebody."

Fear carried us wildly down the trace to tell. Glancing backward over one shoulder I saw Old Indian Wood Chopper coming on down carrying Boy gathered up in his arms. We left all the colors of the world, turnip white and turnip blue, among oranges and heavenly blues and that awful red, of bubbles that burst and ran in fine trickles.

"A sun beam. A sunbeam. I'll be a sunbeam for Him." We had sat together on the bench, and the traveling teacher had instructed us. We sang the songs. Boy's voice, thin and high, came over the top of ours and stood out by itself. "A sun beam. A sun beam. Jesus wants me for a sunbeam."

There were sunbeams sifting through the leaves on top of that high ridge, but Boy was not turning fast into a sunbeam with all that turnip blue and the red hemorrhage.

Sunbeams and stars today are all mixed up with Boy, somehow.

Later, a black cloud covered the sun, then opened, and rain streaks swept up the ridge.

I peered behind the trees watching for those unseen things that attended the day, for I was well aware of their presence.

Old Crow stood motionless, across the Hollow, on a high ridge, watching the consignment. Motionless, she stood, and I saw the wind that came ahead of the rain flap her skirts, but she never moved.

I heard the rain coming upon us. It crossed the Hollow in long black streaks. It struck the leaves, and had I not been watching its approach, but had listened only, as it beat on the leaves, it was like a thousand blackbirds chattering, when they light to feed.

I shut my eyes. I had to, for the water was running down and blinding me. It was like heaven opened up and wept and wrung out its tears. The tears hung on the leaves and grass, and rolled over Old Preacher's face and clung to the end of his nose, which protruded heavenward, and fell in our eyes and ran off hats, and pasted Little Jesus' hair like a cap of long black thorns.

Old Preacher would not stop, but intoned louder and louder with his face turned up toward heaven. For it was his duty, the old custom, to pray the deceased right through the pearly gates.

Some of Old Preacher's words are still with me. I believed then, and still do, every word he said:

"A little lamb is returning to the fold. Receive him, Lord, unto Thy bosom. Grant us to follow his footsteps to the foot of Thy throne. Take us by the hands and lead us. Should danger come nigh, take us under Thy shielding wing. Send us the Comforter; grant us the Grace; do not let the Holy Spirit depart from us. Open up the pearly gates and let this little one who is pure and perfect approach Thy throne. Give to Little Boy a pair of golden wings. Let him be one of the stars to grace heaven, and remember us to Thee."

Old Preacher said, "Amen," three emphatic times.

Then the rain paused and passed on up the ridge. I shut my eyes, and a thousand black birds passed farther and farther away until they were completely gone. I opened my eyes, and there was the ring of clods raked down from the small mound.

We got our breaths again, and there was an awful pause where the air was washed clean in a sodden world and we, ourselves, were sodden.

Old Preacher did not usually run out of words and after the tardy pause called out another "Amen," just like he had forgotten to say one.

I began to concentrate on a droplet of water still hanging to Old Preacher's nose. He wriggled his nose like a rabbit and disposed of the clinging rain. This was interesting to watch and changed my mind from the solemnity of the occasion.

"Why can't I wriggle my nose like a rabbit," I wondered as I turned away.

I felt Old Preacher behind me, before his hand closed on my dripping shoulder.

"Little Boy, he's just like the worm goes in your chestnut." Old Preacher was feeling hungry, I thought. "Little Boy going to sleep all wrapped in his cocoon. Going to see hisself pretty like he's never seen hisself before. Coming out a butterfly. The little worm sees hisself a butterfly, he's never seen before."

Standing around became awkward, so people began to shake themselves and move out.

Marnie tried to bring things back to normal and break the awkwardness by motioning us to follow him down the trace.

Looking wooden faced ahead, he said out of the corner of his mouth, "Damned old long-winded preacher can drown in hell for all I care."

We were to avoid this spot and not to come again soon. Departing, I could hear Old Preacher's assurances, "Litte Boy died satisfactorily."

The traveling peddler always came in the fall. His cart was full of bags of feathers, goose eggs, and many things, but this year he had memorial pictures. He had ways of knowing of deaths. He stopped before Old Indian Wood Chopper's cabin and down came Old Indian Wood Chopper bringing yellow pumpkins, and he looked at the memorial pictures. He made trip after trip back up the narrow steep path and returned with more pumpkins, a sack of walnuts, and of hickory nuts and hazelnuts, to finally bring a small bag containing ginseng roots. The peddler knew the value of delays in trading, but the ginseng was as precious as gold itself, so the peddler said he could have the memorial picture.

We gathered around to watch as the picture was fully exposed and the peddler began writing the name on the tombstone. He brought out various pencils and paraphernalia and someone told him to put the *d* on and spell it BOYD.

So BOYD was printed with fancy curlicues in strange letters on the white tombstone, an angel on either side, and weeping willows and white dove birds and the big sun in the back, with long rays reaching out from earth heavenward. It was a grand memorial picture, but I never saw it anymore for Old Indian Wood Chopper carried it up the path and into the house and closed the door, and I supposed it was for Old Crow, on account of the nuts and pumpkins being hers.

The cart and peddler went on, and I could see yellow pumpkins on top of the bags of feathers as long as I could see the cart.

A storm uprooted the apple tree that was the home of some flickers. The chips flew for several days, and then the mother flicker deposited some eggs in the hole.

"Why is she building so near the house?" This puzzled us, but later, we were to know.

I held her in my hands by stealthily covering the hole with my hand so she could not fly out. Then I lifted her out. Her little heart almost burst, and fear came out in juices around her eyes. We spread her wings and looked at her red spot, then released her to fly away. In and out the parent birds flew while we kept count of the eggs.

Then tragedy struck. It was in the air that day we returned from off the ridge trace. Tragedy had visited. But where? It was in the awful stillness. The terrible battle had ceased. A victorious blacksnake half hung from the hole in the tree, gorged with young birds. One bird was a knot half way down the blacksnake's length. His mouth stretched with another. The snake had lain on the others, crushing them to death. Not quite all — just one was left. Poor naked creature. In fury we beat off the snake and killed him. Then one by one we lifted out the poor flesh. The one, we took to the back porch. He was wobbly at first, but certainly alive. What could one do with a flicker?

"Give him back to his mother. Put him in his nest and maybe she will come back and care for him." She did just that. Poor beaten mother.

Together we reared a delightful creature, who was our joy. The mother carried in the food until he was able to stick his claws in the sides of the hole and look out on the world. We talked to him. We loved him as a dear one.

After a time he sat in the door of his house in the sunlight hours. He talked to us and hollered for us if we got out of sight. We took him down from his hole in the tree and let him walk on a naked spot in our backyard. But walking was not for him. His tail dragged in the dust and served him better as a prop to cling to the bark on the side of the tree. So we let him walk back up the tree to his nest.

Best of all he liked chunks of fat meat. We carried them out of the kitchen from the soup bean kettle to the tree. Then came blackberry season and down his open mouth we poked nice juicy blackberries.

The last day arrived too soon. I had just poked a hunk of fat meat down his guzzle. He gave a certain call which seemed to say, "The world is my apple." He flew to the top of an elm tree. We followed and tried to shake him down to carry him back to his home. Surely he was not ready to venture on his own.

We coaxed him. He returned our calls joyously and sailed around the hill out of sight. All that summer and early fall, the flickers sailed around the hills calling back and forth to each other. We could only listen and wonder if one were ours. Would he ever come back to his old home? Then the storm uprooted the tree. The call of a flicker, after fifty years, brings a nostalgic surge in my heart, and I lift my head with an ear turned listening.

On the road to West-by-God-Virginia, Marnie amused himself with the clouds of butterflies that always followed in season the wagon trace. He saw the patches of blue that were tiny blue butterlifes settled over the horse tracks. Marnie's sharp old-young eyes knew that underneath the lovely heavenly blue the horse tracks were full of horse urine.

I am glad he was wise. Possibly the road led to good fortune, not like the bad-luck egg buried under the oak tree.

"Goodby, Marnie. Maybe the eggs in West Virginia won't be bad-luck eggs."

I paid one visit to Marnie's cabin after he left. I was lonely and felt something to be lost forever. I peeped in through the window. The dirt floor was swept clean, his pallet bed was neatly made. Even the ashes were swept from the hearth. The air hung immaculate. I think I went for the bearskin child's coat. It was not hanging on the peg by the door.

The day came when I knew that I was to go away to school. I stood under my own special tree, my golden catalpa, the tree that since childhood I had sat under and lived under until its familiarities became a sort of second self. I had pulled at its branches, had had conversations with it and with myself. I had stood in its golden shelter, up to my knees in its golden leaves, and looked upward into its golden deeps.

Holy Spirit

Old Rellar had thirteen miscarriages and she named all of them. Only of late, she got mixed up and missed some. This bothered her.

She looked toward the iron bed. It had always been exactly the same. First, came the prayer, then the act with Old Man gratifying himself. Old Rellar heard little of the prayers.

Always it came to nothing. It was like Old Man said, "You live all your life to work things up to come to nothing."

For so many years it seemed all Old Rellar's life, it had been so. Thirteen times she had almost come to term. Thirteen times came the approaching signs of miscarriage.

First came the kidney ailments with their burning pains. She grew to know what was coming.

Once the pains caught her down by the rosebush. She named that one Rose. Again she miscarried in November, and by mistake, named the child October.

Under the steep hill was the spring seep. Water was scarce because it had to be carried uphill by hand. Old Man was not particular. When he wanted a drink he dropped on his knees and blew the green scum aside and drank from water caught in the cow's track.

Old Rellar named that abortion Carrie, to remember being caught as she carried two full buckets of water uphill from the spring.

As other miscarriages occurred she named them after the place of birth or after the season — April, Turnip, Summer, Sunlight, Holy Spirit . . .

Old Rellar loved the sunlight. A spot fell in the middle of the floor where the yellow cat curled and slept.

"I careful to step over the spot. It might be the cat," she said.

The sun shining through the window struck different spots in the shack, telling the seasons of the year. If the sun lay on the flat-topped iron stove she used for cooking, it was winter; in the fall, the sun lay on the iron bed; in summer, the sun struck directly in the middle of the floor.

It was here in the middle of the floor that she fell when the wrenching pains struck. Between black periods, after what seemed hours, she pushed and strained until her body relieved itself of that part of her, which afterwards she referred to as Sunlight. "I name you Sunlight," she said softly, before she arose from the floor, and weakly walked toward the bucket she had used before.

Long ago, since that first time, Old Rellar had learned to wait on herself. The pains brought streaks of blood, to issue forth with her broken waters. In the finality, she felt with her fingers to break the umbilical string. Then with both hands she pushed and bore down on her lower abdomen to expel the afterbirth. She tried to look closely in the mass to discern whether the name should be that of a boy or a girl. Most often she could not tell.

"Gather up the mess and bury it so the hogs won't eat it," Old Man said, pushing a bucket toward her. Then he turned his back and went to stand in the door.

Old Man, feeling sorry for himself, said, "The sun don't s'pose to shine on the same dog's ass all the time."

Old Rellar saw Old Man go for the shovel which leaned against the shed. He would take the bucket, and head up hill toward the knoll where the poplar trees stood. There were graves of all her other miscarriages.

She thought she had done the best she could by her young'uns. She had stood field stones upright to mark each grave. Visiting the graves she passed each one, bending over and tending them buried there, in order of birth behind the poplar trees. The graves on the little knoll overlooked a small marsh in which tall reeds grew supplying the need for coffin measuring sticks to measure the dead. Others had come for the reeds, but there was no need for reeds to measure Old Rellar's misfortunes.

Old Rellar was always the first to arise from her bed in the morning. To begin the day, often she looked toward the knoll.

In the springtime, before the weeds grew tall and when the ground was covered with violets, Old Rellar slipped away from the shack, climbed to the knoll and walked from stone to stone, murmuring, "October, Sunlight . . ."

In autumn time, she thought it pretty to see the sun shining through the naked poplars. For a brief time, their yellow leaves covered the ground in gold, making a golden carpet. Her hands stirred among the leaves, obscuring part of the graves.

It was in the winter that she worried over the cold and was glad when the snows came and blanketed each grave.

"Now, Spring, April, Carrie . . . you can sleep warm. You have a warm blanket."

Only one of her children had lived a night and a day. Too weak to suckle, it lacked the strength to hold with its mouth and draw out the milk. Old Rellar scarfered it with a knife, making a cross on its tiny shoulder, trying to get a drop of blood to put in the blue puckered-mouth, tiny as a rosebud.

"I name you Holy Spirit. It is somebody in Old Man's prayer," she said, hoping to bring good luck to a little boy. She saw his genitals perfectly formed.

There was no death gasp, just a tiny escaping breath like a lost whisper.

She wrapped Holy Spirit close and held him to her for warmth, but it was no use. He was so cold. With him in her arms she walked toward the porch, and stood in the door.

"Take him up with the others," she said to Old Man, not disclosing his name. Just this tiny part, his name Holy Spirit, she would keep for herself.

Old Man rose and stretched and took plenty of time. "I been looking at the flies on the dog's pecker," he said. "A man gets tired toting his treads in a slop bucket." He watched a groundhog come out. Sniffing for sweet cunt, he thought. Feeling injured he took Holy Spirit uphill to scoop out a hole to cover him up before the hogs got at him.

Still standing in the door, Old Reller saw the dogwoods in white bloom among the poplars. Their whiteness was spreading, leaning away from the poplars, making a white skirt. The white bloom was like the nice white cloth she wished for to bury her dead in.

"Holy Spirit, the dogwood is yours," she said and assigned somewhere from her being, the dogwood tree to a little boy, for his very own.

Old Man came down off the knoll, and went to lean the shovel against the shed. He brought back to the shack a piglet wrapped in his coat. Someone had given it to him, thinking it would die.

"You got no young'un. Let the pig suck. Nurse him. It going to die without no drop of milk," he said.

Old Rellar did not want the pig to die. Her one good breast was strutted, swollen, tight and sore. The second breast was withered and spoiled from an old miscarriage. The pig's teeth were needle sharp, and she pulled back sharply, but only briefly, for as the pig began to draw out the nourishment, relief came to her distended breast. There was no indignity. Only the sharp milk teeth of the pig and its powerful suction. The piglet would live and come winter would sleep under the floor of the shack.

The shack was not a cabin built of logs, but was built of clapboard, weathered gray, with the timbers running horizontally. A stove pipe ran out of a hole cut in the side of the shack, for the flat-topped cooking stove inside.

"That kind of stovepipe will burn you down," more than one passer-by had told them.

Behind the shack was the ever-present odor of human feces, for out-houses came much later to the Appalachians. The feces lay and dried or were absorbed into the earth with the rains. Often the feces were eaten by a few bedraggled white chickens who roosted on a pole in the cow's shed, shedding their mites and lice over the cow, the pig, or anybody who chanced to touch the pole.

Bunches of shamey-weed grew near the shed.

"Shaming you for no young'uns," said the Old Man.

When Old Rellar walked close to the shamey-weed, she felt it was so, for the weed seemed to close up and pull away from her as she passed by.

The land was the Old Man's. God knows nobody else would want it. Brush, rocks, briars, at the end of nowhere.

At one time, the shed belonged to the brindle cow; lately to her bull calf. The cow's hill rose sharply from the shed. Now, on top of the hill, lay the brindle cow's bones, bleached by the sun, picked clean by circling buzzards. Her bull calf bawled down by the shed.

"You will have to do without milk someway," said Old Rellar, as the calf nuzzled and tried to eat her dress.

Old Rellar recalled the bull calf's birth. The cow's birthing pains caused her to climb, between pains, to the high hilltop to born her calf. Old Rellar followed the cow and found her with her head stretched straight ahead. Old Rellar saw that with the final heaving contraction the cow had laid her head down straight ahead gently and did not raise it again. The calf had managed to get to its feet and stood by the side of the dead cow on trembling legs with no drop of the first milk.

"I carry you down," she said and with both arms she gathered the calf and started down hill, stopping and resting at intervals to get a breath and a better hold.

"You are not a day old," she said as the wet umbilical cord hung down and became entangled.

"I will boil the corn meal and maybe the milk of the corn will come back." Later she had wet her fingers in the mush and put them in the calf's mouth. He responded at once. He needed to suck. Older, he licked the meal. She stuck his nose into pans of water until he drank. He had survived, but his growth was stunted and he continually bawled down at the shed.

"Damned old turkey buzzards," said Old Man as he flailed his hat about.

Old Rellar watched the buzzards. When she decided to toil up the hill to see the cow, she was unusually slow. She liked the cow and claimed her as her own. She saw one leg bone pulled down hill where an animal had dragged it. She could hear the cow's bull calf down in the shed.

"No good. A tease water," Old Man said.

Certainly the calf would never grow. Round like a cabbage, he stood on stilt legs, with his skin too tight.

Old Reller thought of once when the cow was lost. She talked to herself. "I was looking for you, lost all night. All night I walked the woods, lost. I sat down once on a rock for a minute, but was afraid of poisonous snakes. I got tangled in blackberry briars and was over a cliff as the morning light broke."

Coming off the hill Old Rellar stopped at the knoll where the graves were. She found the Murray Boys had been there and had picked up the grave stones and rolled them down the hill.

"Now, nobody knows where anybody is buried." She made keening sounds and walked toward the shack.

Behind the shack were the frog holes, becoming, in time, rat and snake holes.

"I don't like four kinds of snakes," said Old Man. "Big ones, little ones, live ones, and dead ones."

Old Rellar remembered someone. It might have been her grandmother, who told her stories about the old people who punched holes in their ears and wore little green snakes in their ears as hoops or rings.

"The snakes circled around their necks and caressed their lips." She still remembered the pretty words.

Old Rellar had seen little green snakes in the trees and felt a kind of kinship. They were so pretty.

When Old Man killed the blacksnake, Old Rellar hurt all over. "It nearly kills me," she thought as Old Man stomped the snake and chopped it with his hoe.

"It is like he is stomping me." She stood silent as one part of the snake was flung across from them and Old Man pranced gleefully about the other half, while the muscles were twitching, quivering, and contracting, seeming to fight with him. It was not over until the head was mashed sideways and one eye pushed out.

Later the snake's mate peeped in her door. There he was with his head raised. She did not want Old Man to kill this one, also. With a little brush, Old Rellar drove him up the cow's hill away from her house. He was troublesome to drive and slid off sideways. Old Rellar was very tired when she got to the top of the hill.

"Stay gone," she said.

Returning she stumbled and fell and felt weak. Getting back to her feet she stood still a long while. Her silent figure became part of the landscape. Old Man saw her standing immovable, a silhouette on top of the hill. "A stump," he thought. He watched to see if it moved and thought it did.

"No stump. Old Woman is standing up peeing," he said. "She can stand up and piss and not one drop wet her."

Soon it was late evening. Old Rellar walked around the house. It was like she was saying a goodbye. She looked at the snake holes and up the cow's hill. As for a last time she looked toward the graves.

"Come tomorrow I will go up and visit," she thought. "Not today, but tomorrow."

She walked over the house like going on a journey, seeing if things were right.

By the stove, by the bed, up into the little half-room in the attic where the snake has left his shed skin hanging over the rafters. She felt like the dead snake skin. She was so tired.

Old Rellar lay on the iron bed as she had all the days of her life, it seemed, waiting for Old Man's prayer to end, waiting to fullfill her duty. There were no protests, no words. She heard little of the prayer at all.

Sometime during the prayer she tried naming her children, but it didn't seem right to her. Worrying, she tried to shift her body on the

bed, but could not from some tremendous weight. Maybe if she imagined the graves and the stones she would not leave out any. The graveyard blurred and grew dim.

"Almighty Father," Old Man's prayer went on and always he began
the same, the "a" in Father a short "a" as in cat. He had prayed since the
time at the river.

"He went in a dry sinner and came out a wet sinner," they said.

"No good to baptize a brute," some said. "Wash a hog and he is still a
hog."

Old Man lay his weight and tried to imagine himself fuller than a
dog's tick. He thought of the bull calf. The truth is, he was becoming
like the bull calf, just a "teasewater." Thinking to place the blame on
Old Rellar, he said, "Feels like laying on quilting frames." Sulking he
rolled off, turned his back and lay curled on his side.

"Have you enough hay for the bull calf?" Old Rellar's voice was
weak, far away.

"Might near," Old Man said.

Old Rellar lay still and heard the rat in the wall. She tried to listen
closely, hoping the snake had not come back. She decided it was the rat
chewing paper for its nest as she heard no slides, slithers, or plunks that
the snake always made. This made her feel glad. She thought of the
graves on the knoll. It had been a long time since she had felt like going
up on the hill. Maybe in the spring when the violets came she would go.
She didn't know how far away was spring anymore.

She ought to get up and finish the patch on Old Man's britches where
the knee was cut out. She did not want to get up. She would remember
to do it tomorrow.

She was not sleepy, but was wide awake and she felt very clear. In
fact she could see in the dark. She could see through the clapboard wall
all the way to the graveyard. The grave stones were replaced. The Murray Boys had not rolled them down hill after all. "Holy Spirit's stone is
whitest and biggest of all," she said.

Now she felt herself rising and it was wonderful. With no effort, she was rising up to the knoll where the graves were, on higher and higher above the cow's hill. She could fly up and down the steep hill where she had carried water from the spring seep.

It was wonderful pleasant to float high and look down on the shack. "So wonderful," she heard herself say. "I can see myself inside, lying on the iron bed."

Old Man put out his hand and felt for the warmth from the flat-topped stove. Why was there no fire built in the stove? Why wasn't Old Rellar up?

He reached to push her out of bed and found a strangeness.

His stocking feet touched the floor, chill without the fire. Walking by the foot of their iron bed toward her, he backed off quickly. Some part of a thought came over him. "Slept the night away with Rellar dead and out of this world."

It was early morning, but he would follow the path downward, seeking help from men who would nail together a wooden box. Their women would come and lay out Rellar.

But first he must go under the knoll to the marsh and get a reed for a coffin measuring stick. "The men will ask for a stick to know how long to make the boards for the box."

The marsh stood under the knoll with tall reeds growing profusely in the wet ground. Leaning to cut a reed, Old Man's foot sank and stuck down into the soggy earth.

At the house, Old Man turned back the folded coverlet exposing Old Rellar's body. In a high necked white gown she lay stretched, so the measurement came easy. Old Man notched the reed.

Old Man looked briefly at her. Her nose was pinched and her mouth, agape already, was blackened. Her hands were brought up to her breast and curled like the claws of an animal.

Old Man knew he had seen the same someplace, as his eyes traveled down Old Rellar's gutted stomach, flattened from her many miscarriages. It came to him.

"Like the old dead she-possum. Her young'uns born dead around her like naked rats." Their mouths had been open in a grimace with nubbin-like teeth, black inside like Old Rellar's now.

"It is like somebody I never knew." Old Man dismissed it all.

"How is everyone?" The man asked as he came near.

"They are all dead or dying." Old Man's answer was true indeed.

"Where do you want her put?"

Old Man named the knoll where the yellow poplars were. "It will do," he said. There was no need to mention the graves of the young'uns. Not now or ever. There was nothing to tell then or now.

Old Man turned and started walking back up the path ahead of the others. He felt sorry for himself, mumbling.

"Old Woman picked a pretty time to die with this morning dew cold and wet as hell and myself about petered out. The sun don't s'pose to shine on the same dog's ass all the time."

The men were coming behind with their shovels. "Old Man rode his old woman to death," they said. The shack came in sight.

Old Man muttered, "You live all your life and work things up to come to nothing."

The bull calf bawled somewhere.

The Jake Pond

The time was of locust blooms, hawbushes, and the hawthorn, all abloom by the Jake Pond.

It was the mating season of blacksnakes, in the dead, dry leaves of last year, all writhing, twisting loops and coils.

And spring vaulted into summer; summer slipped into fall, making cycles like the circles left on the face of the pond, where insects lighted, or the boy tossed a pebble out.

The cycles of the seasons were like the tracings left on the pond's banks by some high tides, when the rains swelled the pond to a fullness, later to recede. The boy on the bank followed some of the tide circles, then stopped to look at his image in the pond where he saw reflections of cedar trees and locust blooms, amid a blue sky, full of tiny, white sheep clouds, changing places and chasing each other.

But the boy was of the moment, like the blacksnakes curling and circling and twisting into hoops, and rolling among the dry leaves, to sometimes enter the pond itself and then stretch into long, black strings, which the boy looked at with interest.

Life in the pond was continuous. The boy picked up a mollusk shell from some pristine time. He whistled, and waiting briefly, received an answer. He put his toe into the water and watched the wrigglers skittle into mud covers. Once a huge white crane stood on one leg; both the boy and the pond stopped breathing to keep the rare and motionless beauty theirs.

A heart weed grew on a small promontory, jutting out a ways into the pond. The boy liked to chew on the heart weed, for the chewing produced much spittle. It amused him to see how far out on the pond he could spit. His white spit sat and floated like the tiny spittle of early morning dew spiders. Sometimes the boy could spit a long ways.

A female deer talked to her fawn up in the cedar thicket. The boy had never seen the deer, but he had seen tracks coming down to the pond's edge. Sometimes he had felt wide eyes upon him from the thicket. He wondered what it would be like to be a deer and live in a thicket. Eventually, he would find small tracks intermingled with larger ones when the doe brought her fawn down to drink.

The boy shook the dust from his trousers legs and thought about his peppermint patch. He could already feel the pungent bite of the mint on his lips, and he sniffed in the direction of the patch to try to pick up the sweet odor. But the air was saturated with the smell of mating blacksnakes and the locust blooms. He turned to walk in the direction of the peppermint patch.

From a shelter, the boy sometimes watched the heavy rainfalls of summer obscure the pond in dark straining streaks, and the boy was part of this. The storm was a fascination as it beat the face of the pond into angry wave caps, and the pond rose to meet the storm as if it were reaching long arms.

Sometimes the pond seemed to urge the boy to hurry. Twilight descended and it was an eerie light. The boy felt he should not ignore the prodding to hurry on toward something unknown.

The mystery of the pond held the boy and he became part of the pond. To say the mysterious fascination bewitched him like a woman could not be true, for the only woman he had known was his mother. Her soft bosom memories and the womb memories were of the essence of the pond, and he sank and floated pleasurably, first in the sky above and again in reflections in the depths of the pond.

His mother called him to dinner, and up the meandering path over the rocks he started climbing. Then he looked backward. He could hear the blacksnakes under the locust trees, as they swished and rolled in hoops and whirls, in the old dead leaves of another season.

He stopped to count the leaves of his holly tree. There were seven; last year there had been five. His grandmother had told him that when the slow-growing holly tree grew tall enough to shade him, he would die. But death was a long time off, and the boy's thoughts did not dwell on it. Nor could he think of the one red berry carried in the bill of some unknown bird and dropped there to begin the tiny wondrous seedling. He reached down and cupped the small holly in his hands. The two newest leaves were pale green with red edging. Next year there would be two more, to make nine. Death owned no part of him.

Some days in late summer the boy felt sorrow as if he had lost some-one dear, but the sorrowful thoughts were brief moments. Indeed, they were only quivers, like the spring trilliums he had seen up on the cedar hill, whose petals dropped at the passing of a butterfly. The pond waited for the moments to pass, sitting blue and still.

Sometimes the boy circled the whole of the pond, walking all the way around it. With a stick he tried to hook and bend toward him some cat-tails he wanted to hold. But he could never bend them quite far enough to touch. He would give up and meander after the dragonfly, for it, too, circled the pond.

It was a season of many dragonflies when the pond became a mirror for the cattails and colored trees, until the hills of fall rose from its sur-face. The boy knocked a milkweed with a stick to dislodge a cloud of blue butterflies.

The dragonflies skipped and skimmered; the eye of a duck looked down from a mile high and saw a sunbeam reflected on the pond.

A boy and a dragonfly, some blue butterflies and a wild duck, each made his own minuscule circle, as life around the pond went on.

Throughout the season, the pond remained steady and still and in-tact, through the eyes of ten thousand springs and summer, mirroring the morning sunlight and each night the moon, in its different phases.

Some seasons were good for frogs. A dry season was good for birds.

The frog ushered in the springtime; a wild goose screamed, and little shock waves shivered over the surface of the pond, like fine wrinkles on a woman's face; the whippoorwill called out his season; the cicada called midsummer; and the mockingbird held a concert from the top of the same pine tree. When summers grew lazy, the hawk circled the blue sky above the pond. Once when a summer rain had washed clean even the air over the pond, the boy and a blue lizard looked at each other. The blue lizard looked from shoulders raised high on very human hands. Sounds broke their studied silence and caused the blue lizard to vanish, taking his hands back under the leaves.

With the cycle of seasons came the cycles of birth, of life, of death, for each of the creatures, as the book of life opened and closed around the pond.

Even in his dreams and nightmares, the boy was never far removed from the pond. Down to the pond, in the black night where the waters were black and white and the center of the pond swirled and gurgled black silver, and where the holly tree had grown into a giant tree, casting long black shadows in the waters, the boy was of the pond and the pond was one with the boy. He dreamed of a dark man on the bank, in the cedars, or in a boat, on the dark surging waters. Bad dreams became a coffin box which swirled in the center. As it swirled, it ended upwards to be enclosed and swallowed, engulfing the boy in the coffin. The dreams, the nightmares, the premonitions, the mysteries, intermingled with illusions and reality, were all in the vicissitudes of the pond.

The pond became part of the winter, too; ice covered the life that was buried in the mud. One small unfrozen hole in the middle of the pond told of warm waters rising somewhere deep in the earth.

The boy's father did not allow him to go out on the ice. Dry sinkholes nearby warned that suddenly bottoms fall out of ponds. The boy wondered: if he squeezed his eyes hard and then opened them, would the pond be gone?

Once the boy had seen a huge fish jump up high in the pond's center, though his father had told him the pond held no fish. But the boy had seen one, and was watchful.

The pond was a book of life with the boy as the learner. As he studied the dirty scum clinging to the pond's edge, the scum broke apart then came together again, with something teeming and alive. By reaching out a hand's length the boy could touch saw grasses. Ferns grew on the cool northern banks. Up the hill were the pines and higher up the inclines were the hardwood oaks. Here was the whole history, the whole life cycle of the plant kingdom, from algae through the hardwoods. The boy was part of all this, but it would be years before he would find it in a book. Here by the pond, the book of life was opened wide concerning the flowering time and the spreading of seed and the falling and bedding of leaves, and the boy was no intruder.

So suddenly it was spring again. The pond was surrounded by blooms and profuse flowering. The reflection in the pónd was another world which received the boy gladly. There among the locust blooms and teeming algae, a boy was finding himself never in penury. Again the blacksnakes were writhing and twisting and mating, all in coils and circles, in the dead leaves from old dry years. The scents of the locust blooms and mating blacksnakes wafted in gentle circles to meet circles of peppermint over the breast of unfathomable waters, of the ever and forever Jake Pond.

The Miracle in Sweet Hollow

Whether the miracle happened to Old Man who died cold sober or whether it happened to Old Woman that Christmas Eve in the barn with the animals, you can judge.

Beforehand were those welfare days when Old Man drank up everything. Many times the caseworker sat in her car waiting for Old Woman to walk out of Sweet Hollow as the whipporwills flew along in the trees, accompanying her. A report had gone in to the welfare office before: Their old stove has the bread box burnt out; they have a broom handle propping up the door. Old Woman came out the first of each month, talking, giving details. Each time she talked about her cow. "Had a bull calf. Me nor the cow can discern any eyeballs." She was undaunted. "Bull calf can suck and grow." Old Woman liked the caseworker. She said, "I am going to learn you a tree from a tree."

Old Man was a drunk. He gave out his tobacco money on the street. He had forty dollars left. Welfare had the police to bring him in. He said, "I owe forty dollars to the Home Loans." Welfare called and he did.

Old Woman brought things to town in a bag to sell. Her three children always came along. They lay down beside the street and went to sleep when they got tired. Nobody could move them, and the police did not know what to do.

Welfare finally decided to commit Old Man. They decided to send letters to each of his seven children by his first wife and tell them. And in this case, the miracle started. The seven children began to write in, send Old Man things, and those who were near came to visit. One wrote from Utah, "I was glad to hear thee was still in the World." Old Man turned over and about the word *thee* in his mind, and pondered on it.

Old Man drank less and less and thrived on all the attention from his younguns. "A miracle," welfare said, and Old Woman went on doing the best she could.

Now the other miracle is not about their bad days and hard times nor about Old Man drinking less, but it is a miracle that took place one particular Christmas night out of their total lives.

The tree was ready, strung with white popcorn and colored chains of paper. "I growed that popcorn," thought Old Woman. "I popped it and strung it with my needle and thread. That colored paper I saved all year for the chains the flour paste holds together."

They all admired the tree, especially the children. There was Bud, the oldest boy, a middle boy, and the youngest who was a girl. Under the tree were the boxes the mailman had left down at the road in the mail box. One box was heavy. "Might be oranges," they said. The children handed the box around, weighing it in their hands and shaking it, until the box someway developed a big hole on one end. Big enough for little hands to reach in come out with a handful of candy.

"Who did this?" teased Old Woman.

"Maybe it was a rat," said the children. They didn't know if they should own up.

"I know who was the rat," said Old Woman as the children laughed.

Before dark Old Man brought in the huge back log for the fireplace. Bud helped saw it from a great fallen tree. The crosscut saw tired his arm, and when his strength gave out, the two other children put their hands on his end and helped him pull the saw through the great log. Old Man rolled it through the snow and finally to the fireplace where its fire would last through the night and throw its rosy glow over the room, the tree, and the bunches of bittersweet on the dresser. Old Man had brought the bittersweet in off a high ridge. On the mantel was the pile of cards. Old Woman set her bowl of potato bread to rise near the fire. But not too near. She turned it around to warm each side evenly. Waves from the growing bread floated about in the room.

"Tomorrow they will come," said Old Man. "They will be here tomorrow." He held a card with writing on the back. "I am thinking of *thee*. I was glad to hear *thee* was not poorly." How far is Utah? Old Man's head dropped as he thought, there in the West, one of mine is one of the Chosen, and he has not forgotten me.

All morning Old Woman had sifted things into a pie, which had made the children run around the table and peek and lick spoons, and sop on the bowl, and crinkle their noses at the wonderful, wonderful pie.

"Maw has baked the devil in the pie." Bud caught hold of the youngest girl and pulled her back. Her eyes doubled in wonder, for she believed everything she was told. The next minute she would forget Bud's teasing words, but fifty years later she would remember, "Maw has baked the devil in the pie."

"Bedtime. Go to sleep. So it will be tomorrow." The children mounted a ladder to their beds up over the room in a half loft. The two boys slept at the head of the bed with the girl wedged down at the foot. They kept giggling and calling down.

Out of hiding Old Woman brought a rag doll for the girl and cornstalk animals for the boys and placed them under the tree. Tomorrow there would be city presents when they opened the boxes.

"I had best go to the barn and see if the barn door has come open. The bull calf may have wandered out in the snow and can't see to find its way back," said Old Woman and slipped out the door with a lighted lantern.

The children called down, "Who went out the door?"

Old Man called back, "It is your maw. Going to the barn. If she catches a reindeer, I'll call you for a ride."

Old Woman's galoshes crunched the snow, already frozen on top. Her lantern cast light ahead. Inside the barn, she looked for the dark outline of the cow and tried to see if the blind bull calf was close by her back. She thought she could see them and the one ewe sheep and its lamb and Old Ram. All were asleep except Old Ram who heard her steps and stood up, a few straws sticking out of his mouth, his black face a mystery in the dark.

Old Woman held the lantern near Old Ram's face. She rubbed her fingers into his two ears, which were soft and warm like a warm glove. "Hello. Are you warm?" said Old Woman. "Where is the blind bull calf?"

"Look behind its mother's back."

"I was afraid it had wandered out and could not see to get back."

Old Ram was standing guard. Overhead the doves talked, moving back and forth on the pole. Old Woman thought the sweet odor of the hay turned into perfume. Old Woman saw in the dimness the lamb near its mother, his black legs stretched straight, his black head turned on his side, sleeping.

Old Ram said, "Besides being very new, the lamb is getting fat on milk. He falls asleep any place. He may be hard to wake."

"Will you be waking him?"

"Yes, at midnight. We will all talk at midnight. But you must go. You must not hear."

"What will you talk about?"

"What our fathers and mothers told us. Wonderful things. From the past, and things to come. Mostly, about the Babe."

"In church today, they told the story of Mary and Joseph and the Babe."

"And the donkey and the camel and the sheep."

The cow had gotten to her feet.

Old Woman said, "I worry about the blind bull calf."

"Do not. He can hear better than any of us what all is said."

"We saw Him first," said the cow. "It is our history. You should go now."

"Why?"

"No one is supposed to hear what we say. We want to hear what the blind bull calf says. This is the first time he has spoken."

Old Woman saw the calf rising to his feet. "Can he discern the light from the dark?" she asked.

"Yes, he can see in the dark."

The ground was getting holier.

Old Woman saw fire in Old Ram's eyes as she took up her lantern.

"There is the star," he said. "Look over the door through that crack."

Old Woman saw the star blinking through the crack over the barn door.

Now Old Ram was nosing the lamb to wake him up. He was hard to wake.

"It is time," the cow said. "Can you feel what I feel in the air?"

In a minute the new lamb would be back asleep. His head drooped. Old Ram stood close nudging him upon his black knees.

The blind bull calf was standing. All were looking his way, listening for his first words.

"The bells of heaven. They ring. It is the angels." It was the bull calf.

Old Woman thought she felt the whirring of wings in the air. I should be going, she thought.

"The angels began descending from heaven an hour ago. They are all over the place." The air grew thick. "They are strapping a pair of starry wings on your shoulders," said the blind bull calf to Old Woman.

"Good. Bull Calf can see things that we cannot," said Old Ram. "Don't stay. Hurry."

Old Woman laughed. "I am going now. Don't go out in the snow. I will latch the barn door on the outside."

As she looked back, all of the animals were kneeling.

Outside, snow covered the hills. Old Woman thought she heard bells ringing faintly from somewhere. Blind calf's angels are ringing them, she thought. She walked over the snow so lightly. "It is like I do have wings," she said. Old Woman was very happy. Happiness and the cold from the snow pushed her along fast, like she really did have wings. She thought she skimmed along so fast. "Like I really do have a pair of starry wings," she said. The very hills were singing.

Opening the door, Old Woman stepped into the room. She lifted the lantern to blow out its light. She listened toward the stairs for the children. She saw the room just as she had left it, with a rosy glow over the tree and Old Man asleep in his chair.

She looked about the room for an angel.

Everywhere there was peace and harmony and love. Here was a home, a man, a woman, and some children, and down at the barn some animals were kneeling.

Wildcat John

Wildcat John, they called my grandfather, because he was a hellfire and damnation preacher. He believed in that burning hell he preached about. It seems ironic that the hell he believed in so fully became his part on this earth, so that he suffered, he agonized, and could find no peace.

"There is no peace. There is one thing, if I could tell it, I would be saved," he would say as he ranted and paced back and forth in his terrible restlessness.

What was it Wildcat never could tell, even to save his soul? What was it that took from him his wives, his children, his religion, his health, his freedom, his very soul? What was it he never could tell?

After Wildcat married Dora he never preached again. "He missed preaching," said a neighbor. What was it he wanted Grandma Dora to confess and she never would? If the two of them murdered Grandma Mandy, they never cheated her out of many days, since Mandy had been too long on her sickbed already.

Dora never hinted at anything. Once a neighbor, referring to some old gossip, said, "Remember that green velvet headband he gave you before Mandy died?" It was Dora's way to turn her head and keep silent.

I am Dora's granddaughter. My mother and I were from my grandfather's second family.

Marvin was from the first family. He hated my mother and once said to her, "They cut up my sheet when you were born."

I stood a long while in that cemetery and looked at their names. JOHN: Grandpa, Wildcat John, with a wife on each arm — Mandy and Dora, buried on his either side, and at Grandpa's feet and marked MARVIN, his only son.

The hillfolks being considerate of kinship knew things I could not ask, due to a certain delicacy. However, I found neighbors knew a lot and guessed at a lot more. Some of the memories and hints like tiny pieces of a puzzle, fit together; some do not. The task I set for myself may become a sad chronicle since I am of Wildcat's bloodline. One can find out things it is better not to know.

Nonetheless, what of their passions, their loves, their sins? The wisdom of letting sleeping dogs lie and refraining from rattling skeletons in closets did not deter delving into whatever it was that ran through Grandfather's life, and those close to him, like wild poison, to bring them to their early graves side by side in that unmarked cemetery, overrun so long by briars and the stock.

Modern drivers through certain parts of Appalachia cannot possibly know how it was in those particular times when perhaps one Ford car per day, braving the dirt turnpike, came to a stop in a chughole, then stopped completely, while the driver got out to remove from the road a boulder, recently fallen from the cliff above. Looking upward the driver could see the rocks overhanging a cliff where pine trees withstood storms to grow precariously. A traveler could easily see that he was where in some ancient geologic time the mountain had broken apart leaving the gap for the road that now led to counties on the opposite side. On the mountainsides were the trails of broken trees and branches where, during night storms, rocks loosened and plunged on a downward journey, leaving their trails for the people to come out the next morning and stand in their doorways and yards, viewing the newest rockslides that, ever afterwards, after rains were followed by avalanches of smaller rocks and pebbles.

Big Clinch still looms over the shoulder of Little Clinch now, much the same as then. Lying at the foot of the mountains are the hills with their buckeyed hollows, overgrown with hazelnut bushes and scrub cedars. The ridges stretch away, rocky, with skeletal arms. On the sides of the mountain were the marvelous chestnut trees. Dotted here and there, their white sentinels stand, ghostly remains of forest fires. Here abound the huckleberry bushes where, after the forest fires, within three years, the patches grow again in profusion. Pickers are wary, for the rattlesnake has a tendency to coil himself under the low huckleberry bushes. The seasons come and go. The river is there and at certain seasons stands so still it mirrors the mountains. As I write, thunder is bouncing like a ball from peak to peak.

Along the river were meeting places suitable for all tastes. Up the river was the swimming hole where local bucks swam and cut didoes, in cutoff overalls, submerging their naked white chests, holding noses to bring up rocks from the bottom of the river.

Down the river at a lower area were the Love Springs where couples spread their picnic lunches on crazyquilts on the ground.

Between the swimming area and the Love Springs were the Sulphur Springs, controlled by Grandfather Wildcat John. The sulphurous waters remain today a permanent reminder of Wildcat's very real hell. Drinking the sulphur water for good health was a fad. The rotten odor from the waters permeated the air so people learned to drink it by holding their noses, for the rotten odor had the same rotten taste. For many seasons this area was controlled by Wildcat John, who each Sunday of the summer season, preached hellfire and damnation in the old styles.

Wildcat must have been quite a show for years at the old basket meeting grounds and the watering holes. No one questioned that Wildcat himself had been slain in the spirit and seen the light. He had seen the light as a young man, when he had told Old Pa that a voice told him to "Go preach."

"No, No," said Old Pa, thinking his son was taking an easy way, "Go plow. Plow. Plow."

"Repent, Repent! Hell is burning fire and brimstone." The sulphur odor from the springs made a realistic setting. The fires of hell were real to Wildcat John. None ever believed any firmer than he in a burning hell. "Sinners, confess. Now." Wildcat John blew sulphurous fumes through his waterfall moustache. "Confess, today." Wildcat set his listeners on such fire that they began confessing and repenting and telling their stories.

Close around Wildcat were his followers like a flock of chickens. On the outskirts were the sinners, the unbelievers, the funsters, the lost, the pushovers. Old Mol was a pushover, a poor man's prostitute. She furnished sex, just for the pushing over — under a wagon, behind the haystack, in the sage grass, in the fence corner, any convenient spot.

"Same old sows." Marvin, Wildcat's son, circulated on the outskirts where he talked out loud and poked fun at weeping repentants saying, "Some has bladders behind their eyes."

Wildcat in his prime threw his arms heavenward and with fierce incantations called hellfire and damnation on all womenfolks who bobbed their hair and painted their faces, like red barns.

"Their mouths look like a possum's ass in pokeberry time." All the congregation sniggered, for they all knew about an opossum's anal region, in the season when the red pokeberry was its main food.

Cigarettes and pants for women were new. Old grandmothers still puffed away on their clay and cobbed pipes.

"You Jezebels," Wildcat got braver. "You whores." He gesticulated and jumped and cracked together his heels and began pointing toward the sinners, skulking on the outskirts. Some sniggered, trying to make fun, but they quietened as Wildcat began describing their cries of torment when singeing in hell. It was only a few years afterwards that one of Wildcat's "heifers" put on a pair of pants and walked down State Street, in Bristol, Tennessee, and got herself arrested and jailed.

"Be screaming worse than Old Panther." Wildcat pointed toward the mountain, and they shifted feet for they all had heard the panther's inhuman scream.

"Cars are the devil's wagon — a whorehouse on wheels." Old Mol was standing on the outskirts. She, among other things, had ridden a car all the way to Blountville, Tennessee, and had made a name for herself when the car she was riding in ran off down the mountain. Grabbing the steering, she held the car in the road until it reached the foot of the mountain safely. The natives had been impressed. Now Old Mol was known for other things.

Old Ben was peeping at her from under his hat to see how she was taking Wildcat's burning warning. It had been a week since he had rendezvoused with Old Mol under the mulberry tree.

"Hope she ain't taking hell too seriously. Getting religion can wait."

Getting religion did make a difference in people's lives. Some drunkards did stay sober; some profaners did not curse for awhile; some dog traders refrained from selling dogs on Sunday; some got it, religion that is, lost it, then next time, got it again.

Old Ben, still peeping from under his hat, thought religion was an inconvenience at this particular time. "I just might walk Old Mol home," he was thinking.

The story had died down about Ole Mol and Old Ben when Old Ben was up in "Old Square's" court on the adultery charge. There had been a lot of horse laughs from a reluctant, short-talking witness who did not want to testify, but who was made to tell what he had seen.

"Well, what did you see?" persisted Old Square.

"Didn't see nothing. Just a pair of white legs sticking up."

The Old Square persevered, "What did you think was going on?"

"Just thought Old Ben was getting him a little piece of tail."

Old Ben did not mind the $2.50 fine Old Square put on him, but it was hard to stand the joshing and the gibes he met at every turn he made.

Wildcat pointed fingers toward the outside of the group, calling names, causing these outsiders to try to stand behind each other, or to move out of plain view behind some shrubs. Since Wildcat knew everyone's name and was never averse to shouting a name aloud, it caused much enjoyment to all, except to the one being named.

"You, Ben. Confess now. Now is the hour. Tomorrow may be too late."

"Hurrah for the devil!" came a mocking voice. For a moment no one knew for sure from where.

"The devil has got hold of that boy. Taught him to throw his voice," someone whispered. That boy was Marvin, son of Wildcat by Mandy.

Marvin mocked Wildcat in the midst of his sermons. As Wildcat blew froth and foam past his waterfall moustache, from somewhere came, "Hypocrite." Then, "Son of a bitch." As Wildcat consigned transgressors to hell, he pretended not to be bothered by the voice which came out of the willow trees, then from out of the hazelnut clump. As he pretended not to hear, he further pretended not to know the owner of the voice. He had to know it was Marvin. He had to know it was his son, and I think he did, always.

No matter whether Marvin mocked Wildcat to show his contempt or to get laughs, there were always those who laughed. The devil included.

"The devil is not welcome here." Wildcat's scream echoed around Little Clinch.

Marvin stomped about the gathering. "That dog-hikey thinks he hung the moon and stars." Marvin thumbed over his shoulders toward Wildcat.

Wildcat had a bottle given to him by a traveling man, who said the bottle contained Jordan water from the River Jordan, in the Holy Land. For those kneeling penitents under conviction or those with whom the Spirit was striving, Wildcat poured a few drops of the water into cupped hands, which the recipients hurriedly drank, then dried their hands in their hair. The bottle of Jordan water, at first, was a large bottle with sparkling waters, but too large and inconvenient to carry to meetings, so Wildcat poured some of the water into small vials. It was a year now since the sparkling waters had turned dark brown.

"Piss burnt brown. That is exactly what is — horse piss!" Marvin laughed like he knew plenty. People dropped their heads and nodded Marvin toward destruction. Mean and wicked as Marvin was, he easily could have made the exchange of the waters, which is probably what he

did. Each time Wildcat would offer his Jordan water, Marvin would
jump a ditch to climb a high rock and hiss, "Horse piss!"

There were hints and whispers about Wildcat's wife who was sick and
getting sicker, and about Dora who was nursing her and had moved her
trunk in. There were those who peeped in windows and watched.

The laudanum kept Mandy sleeping at night. A drop or two extra
seemed to stop her continuous fretting and hold her quiet for a long
while. Laudanum was plentiful in the house. Peddlers carried supplies
to the trading posts where it was dispensed freely.

Twilight rising out of the hollows descended to the cabin. The air was
soft under the gold of a full moon, without any whisper of sin and death.

Wildcat and Dora stood in the doorway of the cabin and watched the
silhouette of two mules standing on a high hill. Wildcat knew one mule
was a horse, the other a mare. Side by side, in a tail to head position,
earlier, they had been switching face flies off each other, with their tails.
Wildcat had watched this mutual accommodation many times, not
knowing how long it had taken for this procedure to become innate,
from their ancient need.

Now Wildcat's need was as ancient as that of the mules. The air was
filled with that need. The mules felt it. Dora felt it. Needs have a way
of rising.

Inside, Mandy lay emaciated and stretched, her hands picking at the
covers. Hands picking at the covers is an omen of impending death,
as everybody knew. Wildcat had looked in earlier and seen Mandy
stretched and relaxed. Now he saw her hands plucking at the sheets.

Dora's trunk was in the corner. She had already moved in. She had
come months earlier to nurse Mandy and do the housekeeping. Neighbors could tell there had been other developments.

"John, come here." It seemed to John that he had heard Mandy call
him a thousand times. In the beginning he had responded, but she had
never told him anything she wanted.

Now, much of the time, Wildcat just called back to Mandy, "In a minute."

That morning as he had carried in some wood and dropped it behind the stove, he turned and saw Mandy's hollow sunken eyes following him. She had said, "John, it won't be long now."

What matter of a drop or two extra laudanum? What of those who need to die and of those who need to be born? Death can be long or short; so can lovemaking. Is lovemaking in a house where there is a death bad luck? Wildcat had heard it was so. Adultery. What of adultery? *Thou shalt not. Thou shalt not.*

The next morning they found Mandy, her mouth agape, like she had gasped a breath.

Wildcat threw back his head and laughed, "The battle is over. The victory is won." These were strange words at a wife's passing.

Someone notified Mandy's two brothers, who came from over the mountain. They were burly men who stood quietly and said, "We want to take our sister's body back home." Wildcat made no objection when they rolled Mandy in quilts and loaded her in a wagon and started toward the gap where the mountain had broken apart.

Dora and her trunk stayed on. Three weeks after Mandy died, Wildcat and Dora married. It obviously was a hurry-up affair for a baby arrived before time.

"Premature," Wildcat tried to say.

"Premature, hell. A full-time baby if ever I saw one," the neighbors laughed.

So Dora was pregnant before Mandy died. She was carrying Wildcat's child.

"What do you reckon?"

"Perhaps laudanum accommodated." The neighbors whispered.

The night the baby was born, Marvin awakened to scissors, in somebody's hands, cutting off the bottom of his sheet. He heard sounds like a cat crying.

"What is somebody doing to the cat?" What a boy couldn't know then, Marvin knew later. My mother was being born, and a baby's bands and necessaries were being cut from the bottom of Marvin's sheet, while he was in the bed.

"Preacher's bees swarmed." The neighbors laughed and bandied an old hill saying.

Marvin listened. He remembered and never forgot anything. When things he heard rancored in his mind, he would flee out into the night terrors, hating Wildcat, himself, everyone. "The son of bitch ort to died forty years before he was born," Marvin told the neighbors.

After Mandy died, Wildcat did not go to the Sulphur Springs again. He never preached again after he married Dora. He must have missed it greatly. Something as strong as steel traps held him back so that he began a retreat from everyone. Never to preach again. Never to feel the call again. Wildcat began to talk about being lost. "Something is bothering him," neighbors said. The old man desperately needed some replacement for his preaching so he turned to his son Marvin. He would *save* the boy.

Marvin had never been any help for Mandy, not even in her last days, as she weakened. He was no help to anyone.

The spring was several yards downhill from the cabin. It was hard to carry drinking water uphill. Marvin came in and looked at the empty bucket, tossed his hair off his brow, and sat down.

"Oh, how I hate to carry water," his mother had said. Carrying water and washing in tubs had long ago taken toll on Mandy.

"Here, you can wear my gloves," said Marvin. Wildcat had made Marvin a pair of little gloves out of the hide of a groundhog.

Hands of mountain women were ruined in the tubs; backs and shoulders gave way to heavy loads; bladders and wombs fell from childbearing. When the women went out into the new grounds and cornfields, a new baby went also. Marvin had been born upon an old quilt at the end of a corn row.

The older Marvin had no notion of carrying water, or hoeing those rows, or breaking the new ground. In the new grounds where rocks hurt bare feet and dewberry briars entangled his legs, he would claim a need to go off into the woods, on a call of nature. He would be gone a long while.

"Been grafting a chinquapin to a servis," he said, returning. "What time is it?"

"About ten o'clock," replied Mandy.

"Do you know why I asked what time it is?"

"No, I figured you just wanted to know the time."

"I'm thinking of quitting. That is why I asked."

"Quitting before you even started," Mandy had wearily replied.

During Marvin's early years, he had raised hell generally. His devilments were well known. He enjoyed such cruelty as tying two cats together over a clothesline and watching them claw each other to death. He drank the sheep manure tea to break out the measles to show what the hell he cared. He rode a horse into the churchhouse. Slogging through the mud in the twilight he mocked the whippoorwill's call and answered, "Whip your wife. Whip her well." Coming in home on late nights, he mimicked a she-panther, tantalizing the panther that followed him along the mountain side. The panther followed him, screaming at a she-panther that had a human odor.

"I'm not afraid," called Marvin to the children, who poked with sticks at the devil's dust bag. Marvin jumped with both feet on the devil's dust bag and flattened to the ground the brown puffed ball, which sent a dark cloud of spores flying into the air. The children were afraid and ran away. The spores blew all the way and settled in a mudhole.

One cold winter, Marvin rebelled against sleeping with Old Pa. Marvin did not care if it was healthful for the old to sleep with the young. He did not care if it was healthful for the old to breathe the breath of the young or if Old Pa was gouty and always cold and talking of dying. What he had against Old Pa, who had come to live with them, was that he was a "a table-robbing son of bitch, eats up all the vittles. Should go on to the poorhouse."

Down in the hills one does not say *bull* before ladies. Ladies don't say *bull* before gents. Marvin said *bull* anytime he felt like it.

There was the story about Marvin and his two cronies going up Moccasin to have a little fun. Some thought what happened funny and laughed. Others did not like it one bit.

They were going to the highest house in the Hollow and work down. They got the old fascinators which belonged to their womenfolks. Dressed in old clothes, they wound the fascinators around their heads, crossed them in front to hang down their backs.

"You be the wife. You be the husband. I'll be the daughter." Marvin, being smallest, was the daughter.

The mountain folks never turned away anyone asking to share the night even though accommodations might be poor, as all living was done in one room. This meant sitting up all night or lying on a pallet before the fire.

"Hello."

"Come on in, folks, make yourselves at home."

"We want to stay all night. This one is my wife and this one is my daughter."

They were made welcome with chairs near the fire. Then the pranking started.

Old Unc Jasp had already gone to bed and his foot-long white beard lay outside the covers.

"Where is your husband, missus?" asked Marvin in a high girlish voice.

"Why, that's him over there in the bed."

"I'm so fond of the men. I'll just have to get a little closer." Marvin, as the daughter, went over to the bed and began to fondle Old Unc's long

white beard. After caressing him, he climbed up in the bed and lay
down beside Old Unc, saying, "Pretty beard. Pretty-pretty."

"Pooty ! Pooty! Pooty!" said the old man, making clucking sounds,
getting more and more excited, until he caught sight of short hair under
the fascinator. He raised with a roar.

"Woman, haven't you had your hair cut sometime? What kind of
woman are you?"

With that Old Unc shoved Marvin right off the bed onto the floor.
Women with short hair were in the same category as cardplayers, hog
thieves, and whores.

"Are you one of them Jezebels?"

"Cut my hair to get rid of head lice." Marvin and his cronies made a
hasty exit.

Word got out about Marvin and his cronies playing up to Old Unc
Jasp and getting in bed with him, and the word was that up at Old
Unc's place, "they didn't like it."

"Marvin has got too much pissaringtum. Needs the hellfire beat out
of him."

Wildcat worried. He was not making much headway with Marvin.
Days turned into months and the years passed by. My mother and her
sisters grew up and left home early. Marvin stayed.

Wildcat looked toward the Sulphur Springs. "There is one thing, if I
could tell it, I would not be lost." He tried turning thought from himself
to Marvin. "The boy must not be lost." He was fighting more and more
with Marvin's reckless bullying.

"Bound for destruction. Possessed of a devil," neighbors said. Marvin's eyes looked wild and he was always watching from the side of the
house. Small, he was quick as a cat.

"I hit at him and he was not there," said a ruffian who had lost a fight.
Strong, he once threw the Law up in a hornbeam tree. His cold blue
eyes became holding, like some monster slipped from the mud. Hating
everyone, he had demons inside ready to jump out.

"He is fated," they said.

"Someone will have to kill him," they said, having no way of knowing that a fifty-year-old mudhole waited.

Wildcat was not having any success with Marvin. He wished Marvin was not so unruly, so surly with him. He tried to tell him funny stores about Old Bal. "Old Bal had a dime in his pocket that fell in the mule's mash, so the mule ate the dime. Old Bal rode the mule backwards for a week until he recovered the dime." Marvin turned his back even when Wildcat told another story about Old Bal. "Old Bal was riding his mule up the steepest mountain ever seen. He had on his overcoat with a big collar on it. That mountain was so steep that the mule done his business right down his coat collar. Now for the question, Marvin; when the mule done his business down Old Bal's coat collar, were they going up the mountain or coming down the mountain?"

Wildcat looked around. Marvin had put distance between them. He screamed, his laughter floating backwards, "You son-of-bitch are running away from God."

It was a bumblebee summer with a buzz in the air. Wildcat thought to take Marvin snake shooting and try to get on the good side of him. Wildcat hoped he could talk to Marvin, this untamed wild son in whom no gentleness seemed forthcoming.

The summer day was warm and perfect for climbing over cliffs and breaking through underbrush. A chicken hawk lazily circled, peering down at the chickens near the house, miniature below.

Wildcat stood on an old log and saw something sunning, something copper colored and spotted, yellowish in his new skin.

"Marvin, come get this copperhead snake. The big yellow one." The snake lay curved about the rocks, looking a foot long.

Wildcat wanted Marvin to shoot the snake, so he held back.

Marvin came crashing through the bushes.

"Aim at his head. Don't miss now," said Wildcat. Marvin aimed and the roar and the bullet sent the snake twisting and curling, a curling and twisting body jerking for its head. Out of the bullet hole rolled worm-like baby snakes. Six of them.

Soon there was a strong odor. Wildcat knew the smell.

"Smell the cucumbers? There is another snake around here. Mate of that one."

Marvin saw the snake. "Over there," he said as he saw the black copperhead open its mouth to swallow the six baby snakes.

Again Wildcat let Marvin do the shooting. A blast made a hole in the black copperhead's side.

"Lookee there!" Wildcat pointed to the baby copperheads piling out of the hole. Only this time he counted twelve.

With a whoop Marvin jumped among the snakes and began stomping the baby snakes. He snarled and ground up the baby snakes under his feet. Bits of flesh clung to tops of his shoes.

"Got me fourteen snakes at one time," Marvin bragged and beat the bush with his gun. "Get the old ones in this sack. We will bust off their shell. Snake meat is the whitest meat you ever seen."

The old man wished Marvin was not so wrought up. "Their wriggling don't hurt nothing. They is dead."

But Marvin was gone, and somewhere from the bushes came, "Hurrah for the devil!"

Wildcat had seen people put their hands on top of their heads and under their feet saying "Hurrah for the devil! Take all of me." The old man was afraid Marvin was ill-fated.

The buzzard's roost was near the bluff over where the mountain broke apart in a little sink among some large trees. On summer days during early mornings, the buzzards sat on the branches of the trees and spread their wings, sunning themselves. Toward late evening hundreds of them winged themselves homeward toward the roost from their carrion. Marvin had visited the buzzard's roost and said the buzzards had ruined it. "Filthy. Not fit to look at. Nastiness, feathers, and bones. The puke will stink you to death."

Early summer brought the red heifer to calving time.

"Gone to the highest ridge. That is their nature," said Wildcat, when he found her missing. He had traced numerous cows and found them on some high point with their calves. For those he could not find, he had waited three days until the mother came down for water, then followed them back to where they had hidden their calves. Wildcat wondered what it was in the cow's nature that made her cause him all this trouble. This time he thought he would follow Marvin. Maybe he could help bring the cow in.

Marvin cruised over several ridges without luck. As he approached the buzzard's roost, he noted much activity with buzzards sitting by two's and by three's on the tree limbs. Others were circling to light upon the ground. Marvin stepped closer and could see their black hulking bodies and their ugly heads with their red eyes. Sprawled upon the ground was the red heifer with two buzzards perched on her side. Nearby was the calf. Dead. Its eyes were pecked out down into their sockets. Marvin's eyes traveled over the red curly haired calf, looking as if it had been licked by its mother's tongue, to the hollow sockets where eyes were missing, on to the black hulks sitting quietly watching him. Marvin furiously began to fight the buzzards with sticks, rocks, anything that came into his hands. Feebly, the heifer raised her head at the ruckus, turning sorrowfully toward Marvin. He saw the afterbirth still attached to the heifer's body and knew why the buzzards were waiting. Death was coming if the cow retained the afterbirth. The calf appeared dry so it had been born some time now. "Bastards," Marvin screamed toward the buzzards.

Wildcat came closer and saw Marvin fighting the buzzards. He approached the mother cow and her calf, noting the cow still breathed. Attempting to lift the cow to her feet, he helped her to stand, though she wobbled from side to side, to lean against him. Wildcat wondered how he could get her home and started encouraging her along the path, until he noted the afterbirth string still attached dragging behind.

Wildcat called to Marvin, "The calf is dead. The afterbirth has not come. You will have to help here."

The old man had removed the afterbirth many times from his own cows and those of his neighbors'. It had to be done here, though already it seemed too late. He saw two buzzards trailing.

Wildcat knew the value of time. Like the time a cow was choking and he plunged his hand and arm down the cow's windpipe and pulled the apple out that was choking her down to the ground in death. As then, now, no time must be lost.

"I have nothing to wash with," said Wildcat. He plunged his hand and arm up to his elbows into the birth seat of the cow until he felt little pegs, over which the afterbirth was hung. The afterbirth fitted over the little knobs and Wildcat felt all around until he loosened the afterbirth from all the pegs. Then he rolled it out.

The cow sank to her knees, then to the ground where she stretched and sighed one long sigh.

"Too late," said Wildcat. "Smell the afterbirth. Already rotten." He wiped his hands on some leaves.

"Come, help cover her," called Wildcat to Marvin, who was still cursing the buzzards and attacking them with increasing fury. Wildcat raked mounds of leaves over the cow's body, which, when weighted down with sticks and rocks, would be little protection against the black buzzards waiting. Already the two who were stalking were advancing, nearer and nearer, their red eyes noting the disturbed leaves. Wildcat knew they would begin at the eyeballs.

Marvin continued to fight the buzzards savagely, rocking them violently from their perches. As if to get even, the buzzards crisscrossed over Marvin's head vomiting strings of putrid filth. "Bastards," screamed Marvin, hurling a rock and striking one, causing it to drop a few feathers. Wildcat watched a black feather, supported a ways in the air, drop toward the earth.

Wildcat was standing still, not moving out of his tracks. He was getting more and more that way. Wildcat was talking to himself. "I will turn the hogs through the rail fence." He was turning the hogs to fatten on the sweet chestnuts. Usually Wildcat noticed the "yar" along the path, for yarrow was a good gout medicine. Gout had been Old Pa's trouble. Here and there was the penny royal. He reached down and picked some "penny rile" and put it in his pocket. The penny royal was good for tea or if hung up in little flour pokes, it would keep flies out of the house. Wildcat was meandering. He was consuming time. He came upon the benjamin bush. It exuded a spicy odor. Wildcat knew the spicewood. He had drunk the spicewood tea. He felt the penny royal in his pocket. It was good to smoke. Marvin liked to smoke it. It made his mouth feel cool and nice. Wildcat thought he would give some penny royal to Marvin.

"Where is Marvin? Been gone for three days, now." Wildcat meandered.

Some neighbors allowed, "He has run off until the corn is laid by. Like he did that time when you needed rails for the rail fence."

The neighbors went on, "We figure he has gone to the turnpike to catch a wagon to ride down to Blountville. Court is setting in Blountville, Tennessee, where they going to try Kenny Wagner."

Kenny Wagner was a desperado who had killed several men, and no jail could ever hold him. Rumors were that Kenny had spent the summer down river in the hills among his kinfolks. There were those who claimed to have seen him and talked with him and they pointed to an old root cellar where Kenny laid low until the Law took him in. If Marvin ever saw him or had any connection with him, it was never told.

Along the way, between wagon rides, Marvin noted many lost horseshoes, turned up in the mud. He would have liked to take the new-looking shoes home to nail over the barn door where he already had some. The old rusty-looking shoes he picked up and flung over his left shoulder. An old saying went, "If you find a horseshoe, make a wish and cast it away over the left shoulder. Then your wish will come true."

So Marvin thought the long trip slogging through the mud worthwhile. When he arrived in Blountville, people were gathered in little knots, swapping knives, and swapping whopping lies. Horses were tied everywhere, getting rested for the long trip back home, filling up their stomachs by sticking their noses into little feed sacks tied to their heads.

The spectators were watching the jailhouse right next to the courthouse. "They will bring Old Kenny out and have his trial in the courthouse," a man told Marvin.

People stretched their necks, for two Laws were bringing out somebody, who, as the people strained to see him, could not have been anybody's idea of an outlaw.

"More like a dirty old man," somebody observed. Marvin followed the crowd into a large room of the courthouse, where there were long benches to sit on. Marvin was to tell many times about his trip and the trial when he got back home.

Wildcat saw Marvin coming back. He was so glad to see the boy, that from the recesses of olden times his speech came out in an odd construction. "If I knowed you had went, I would seed you had a way."

Wildcat would have laid his two hands on Marvin's shoulders but Marvin would have none of him and shrugged him off sideways. They were near the mudhole, where in the night, a miracle had happened. Hopping about were thousands of tiny frogs.

"It rained frogs in the night," said Wildcat to Marvin. To show his contempt for his father, Marvin yelled and jumped into the mudhole stomping the tiny frogs, crushing them each time his foot came down.

"No need doing that," said Wildcat, who could hear the flesh crushing under Marvin's foot. Wildcat did not like the way Marvin was stomping.

Marvin had no notion of giving Wildcat details of his trip, but Marvin had a good story to tell to others.

"Sentenced to die for murder. What do you have to say to that?" the judge had asked Kenny.

"You don't know clean shit from applebutter." Marvin heard Kenny say it. It made his trip worthwhile to have it to tell when he got back home. It was told and retold and is told to this day, plus it is to be found in the court records at Blountville, Tennessee — how Kenny Wagner defied that judge, and death, and spit right on that courthouse floor.

Wildcat stood in his bare feet in the doorway. He heard the four o'clock
wind in the timber on the high ridge. The wind always blew with great
velocity at four o'clock, each day. Wildcat had observed it for fifty years
and it had never failed. In a few minutes, the cold wind would come off
the ridges into the hollows and coves. Wildcat rubbed one foot on the
other, already cold.

He looked down toward the cow meadow where a flock of blackbirds
was rising from the corn stubble and settling among the black droppings from the cattle. All night the cattle had lain and had left some of
the corn they had eaten, whole and undigested in their droppings. Now
the blackbirds were eating the corn. Wildcat did not like to see the
blackbirds. He had heard they meant bad luck as well as rain. He
looked toward the clouds. "I wish I knew where that boy is."

He wandered off past the chestnut grove. Later in the night, he heard
the wind blowing the limbs to thresh against each other and make a
knocking on the ground. "I'll gather my hat full of chestnuts and call
Dora to come fill her apron." He heard the hogs eating among the underbrush. Up a ways was the indian peach orchard, which Marvin
liked to visit, getting mouthfuls of the red peach juice and spitting it out
like a tooth bleeding. The knotty, wormy peaches he would spin against
the cliff wall.

Wildcat listened but he could hear nothing of Marvin. He would
walk far enough to see if Old Bear had been in the huckleberry patch.
He gathered some cane seed to take home to poach, to grind up, and to
boil into a kind of coffee. He felt colder.

Turning homeward, he thought of when Marvin was born to Mandy
and him, and of his pride. "A preacher. A preacher like me," he had
thought. The night of Marvin's birth, a violent March windstorm
played havoc with the trees and small buildings. Mandy had called in
the night to say it was time to go fetch the midwife. Getting back, they

found Marvin already arrived and screaming, as he was to scream, letting no one rest, for six months. Marvin had been different always. It was like the storm had entered the infant. He would never knuckle under. He was the wild cow the farmer could never handle and had to get rid of. He fought and cussed when he was little, just as he fought and cussed when he was older. Wildcat remembered the storm and how the weather had changed when they took the midwife home. A murderer's moon was out, all red and ugly, making the midwife say, "A murderer's moon is not a good moon. Should better have been a strawberry moon."

The old man stopped and stood in the yard and looked at the bluff where the wind was moving the limbs of the pine tree.

Wildcat looked at the trees and flying clouds. "Where is Marvin? Marvin might be up on the bluff in the storm. I wish I knew where that boy is. God, is Marvin to be lost, too?"

A man was coming hurriedly into sight. Wildcat stepped to meet him.

"Come quickly," the man began calling. "It is Marvin. He is killed. Name o'God."

Wildcat and the man broke into a run, and he and the man came to where a few men were moving something around near the big mudhole in the road.

"Marvin is killed. Done dead a'ready. Plumb dead he is. Name o'God." One of the men came close to Wildcat. "He picked a fight with three of them. They run off that way, down the road."

Wildcat saw what the men had pulled from the mudhole, all caked with yellow clay mud, with the men stripping off the clothes and washing him down with buckets of water drawn from the creek.

Wildcat saw a bleeding place in Marvin's breast and the black bruises over all his body.

"They cut him with a knife. They stomped him in the fifty-year-old mudhole. When he was dead, they said, 'Let's give him some more,' as they rocked his body."

It was over. Wildcat knew.

When the men saw Wildcat was attempting to lift the body into his arms, they asked for a sheet from a woman standing nearby. She brought it from her cabin, and the four got hold on each corner and they turned toward home.

The old man walked frozen behind the body, saying no word.

In the growing late twilight, the orange of the autumn foliage lit up the side of Little Clinch, lit the world aglow, suffusing over it a burnished light. The sharp black shadows of the men carrying the body jerked along like puppets on a string, in the eerie light.

Oh, the ruin. To be stomped to death in a fight, his head wet and ruined in a fifty-year-old mudhole.

Now who would ever understand if looking at the yellow maples on the side of the Clinch meant anything to Marvin?

Or if he had thoughts of living and dying gloriously like Kenny Wagner?

Who would ever know what he wished for with the lost horseshoes he threw over his shoulder?

Wildcat did not lift his head to look at the mountains ever again. Now it had all fallen on him.

"I accept the blame. The blame is on me." The men heard him choking, and stepped faster. The gloom that had settled over the cabin had lifted, but the mist had turned into a phenomenon. It was raining in the moonlight. Raining gold.

Dora saw them coming and held the door open for them to lay the body on the bed. She held a quilt to cover it. Dora wondered why the body was naked for she did not know about the mudhole. She could tell that Marvin was dead and knew her job would be to get his clothes for burial together. A full set would be required down to the white socks.

A man stayed to cut some wood, while the others left to give word of the need for a pine box, and for assembling a grave-digging crew that would climb to the highest hilltop the next day with their shovels to dig out of the clay, six feet deep and four feet wide, a new grave.

Soon food would begin to arrive from cupboards and cellars as each neighbor heard the news. By late evening, friends and kinsmen would begin to arrive to stay the night.

The old man stumbled to the doorway of his cabin. He looked at the pine tree waving its branches high on the escarpment over the cliff. The rain which had started gentle seemed to be turning into a storm. As he stood, it became fierce enough to send a tree tumbling down the cliff. Wildcat felt broken apart like the mountain. He watched the storm worsen. He walked out into the storm to stand, begging the rain to wash him clean. He implored the eternal night to cover his transgressions. Marvin's sins were his. He accepted all.

A wild inhuman cry, starting as a moan, tore from him, loud enough to waken the mountain panther, as Wildcat begged the lightning to strike his troubles and separate them away from him like the boulders falling down the cliff.

"Beat me, storm. It cannot be this way. What I preached is true. I have seen the light. I have been slain in the spirit. Where are you, God? My son — to be lost, I cannot bear it. Confess — I cannot. I am lost. Take me quickly, God, out of this valley of hell. You see, I do not forget you, God."

Wildcat exposed his breast to the storm. The fires from that hot torturous hell he preached about were now burning him, and his soul was suffering the pangs as his body was being consumed.

"Confess," rang out every way he turned. Wildcat knew what he had to do but he could not do it. "Let Marvin's sins be on me. I am lost. I do not want Marvin lost."

"You cannot bargain with God." Wildcat heard this from somewhere as he began clawing at the cliff. As he climbed it, he hoped to be killed. "Devil, take me quickly." On the top on a flattened rock, he prostrated himself and let the rains drench him until a kind of unconsciousness overcame him. He awakened like from a cold dream.

"Lost. Lost in the world to come. Not to be awakened in the haven of rest. My boy. My boy. Me, but not my boy. Devil, couldn't you be satisfied?"

In the morning light, Dora saw him coming in home, not disoriented, but seemingly contrite and docile.

"I have already died and this is hell." He appeared lucid but as a man without hope — hope for whatever there is, in immortality.

Dora handed him the pair of white socks, handwoven from fine sheep's wool, and they moved toward Marvin's feet. He lifted the quilt and saw that Marvin's feet had already turned black. The feet looked small, almost girllike. On each stiffened foot Wildcat drew gently the white socks.

After Marvin's death, Wildcat began acting queerly. He talked to himself. He peeped from behind trees. He looked in church windows during service. He would sit and look at Dora for long periods of time muttering, "How are you going to like burning in hell?" Dora would have to rise from her chair and have business in the kitchen. Hunters in the woods suddenly came face to face with him out of nowhere. He walked and rode restless and was never content to stay in one place.

Dora awakened one night with Wildcat standing over her bed.

"Are you going to hurt me, John?" she asked.

"You know I never would hurt you, Mandy," said Wildcat, as his old wife's name slipped out.

Dora got advice from some of the neighbors when she expressed her fright. Their opinions did little to allay her fears, for they had all observed Wildcat walking the meadows.

"He mumbles, 'Mandy, Mandy' or 'Marvin, Marvin,'" they said. "He is dangerous. He might kill somebody. He has lost his whereabouts. You might ought to send him off."

Dora agonized about putting Wildcat away. "It is the hardest thing I have ever had to do. I do not want to do it." She made last-minute everyday appeals to Wildcat from old wifely concerns. "You ain't chewed no tobacco all day. You ain't got your old hat on."

Wildcat turned fiercely upon her. "Woman, is my name not to be written in heaven?" His mental deterioration affected him physically as he retired more and more into a dark world apart with that something that bothered him, causing his mouth to be dry, and causing him to lose continence as evidenced by his trousers showing wet at times. Neighbors influenced Dora's reluctant decision to have Wildcat committed to the Marion asylum, some thirty miles distant.

"How will we take him? He will be hard to capture," neighbors said.

"I don't want to go the asylum. I will not be taken. I am going into the mountain." Wildcat appeared at a neighbor's house, wet in the early morning dew, his eyes wild.

"Eat your breakfast before you go into the mountain." The neighbor hoped to delay him, for he knew the sheriff was on the way.

"I am going up the cove into the mountains." Wildcat mumbled and trembled. No one knew the mountains better than Wildcat, and the Law might have considerable trouble ferreting him out. Wildcat declined breakfast and vanished into the trees.

There were days with no luck until the Law walked upon him hiding behind a rock. They took him and handcuffed him. They brought him out of the mountain, scratched and bleeding, his bony wrists mangled from the cumbersome, outmoded handcuffs.

A neighbor said, "I could of brought him out myself in better shape. You Law are a bunch of yellow cowards."

Dora stood crying and rushed to wipe his bleeding wrists with her apron. In the strange aftermath, a tale was told that Dora never washed the apron or threw it away, but kept it fetishlike and was seen holding it on her lap and crying into the blood spots.

Wildcat went with the sheriff, docile enough. He seemed lucid, saying quietly, "If I could tell one thing, I would not be lost. I am lost. There is one thing I cannot reveal."

For months Dora visited at the hospital, paying neighbors to drive her there at considerable expense. The speech Wildcat always made must have been embarrassing.

"Peace. Peace. There is no peace. Not even to save my soul."

On Dora's last visit, three years after he had been brought there, he pointed an accusing finger saying, "Woman, you are the cause of me being here." About a month later, his lungs, nurtured on mountain air, and his muscles, strong from climbing Little Clinch, let go of his tortured soul as the breath stopped for no reason in his throat and finally ceased. The nurse, who knew the death rattles, waited a few moments. Then she drew the cover over his face. "I do not forget you, God." The nurse reported these were his last words.

Something like doom descended the mountain and lay around the cabin. Dora walked away from the porch. She rolled down her sleeves to cover her arms and rolled up her hands in her apron. She met some neighbors walking in the road. She spoke, "I heard John come into the house. Three times I heard him drop the wood behind the stove. John is coming home today. I need somebody to bring him." The sheriff's car had transported him fast, but the neighbor's horse-drawn wagon would take long hours to bring him back.

Wildcat came home in a pine box and lay a corpse. There was to be a wake with singing and eating, lasting the entire night. Women, recently widowed, were always closely watched, as stories were told of how so-and-so, weeping, looked through fingers, across the grave, and picked out the next spouse. There were other reasons why all eyes were observing Dora. What would she say? Would she break down? Maybe she would confess?

Word was passed that Dora wanted everyone to go home at midnight. She was sending her daughters home and refusing the company of neighbors. To break the custom of having an all-night wake was a strange procedure, even a disappointing one, but there was nothing to be done, except for the inquisitive merrymakers to begin to disperse.

After the neighbors left, it was quiet, the perfect peaceful quiet, enfolding the dead. The lamplight cast its shadows on the wall, and darkness hovered in the corners. Outside, the darkness embraced the cabin, shutting out a few watchers who had come in close, to peer in at the window.

The lamplight fell upon Dora's hair. These last years it had become streaked with white strands and thinned, where once its luxuriance fell below her waist. Some women bragged they could stand upon their hair; Dora could sit upon hers. She loosened her hair as for combing and walked toward a chest of drawers, purposefully.

As was the custom, any woman worthy of the name, kept her burying clothes, a full outfit down to the white socks, wrapped and ready in a bottom drawer. From the lowest drawer, Dora took something in a little box, which as she held it out and up to the light shone gold like a ring. A small darkened bottle definitely was a laudanum bottle. Another bottle might have been an old perfume bottle, but the faces watching through the window recognized a vial of the Jordan water.

These articles Dora removed from their careful wrapping in an old soiled apron covered with dark spots like blood. She moved with them toward the pine casket box.

She attempted to straighten Wildcat's hands but found them stiffened from the shoulder, so she replaced them on his breast. Then uncorking the vial of Jordan water, she poured the contents over Wildcat's body. Afterwards, she wrapped the ring, the laudanum bottle, and the empty vial back in the soiled apron and pushed them under the clothing in the casket box, out of view.

Last, she took up a vigil sitting on a straight chair, her unmoving shadow becoming one of the tall shadows cast on the wall by the lamp. All the night she seemed oblivious to the old rat in the wall, scratching in his fur, and to the settlings in the casket box.

The last time I saw Grandmother Dora, she was dried up and so very old, but sitting straight in an old-type straight chair. She had lasted and lasted, forgive me, and could not die. She was very small with yellow skin stretched over the contours of her face. I sat by her side, as small as she, and called her name, "Grandmother."